JESSICA BECK

THE DONUT MYSTERIES, BOOK 27

FLOURED FELONIES

The First Time Ever Published!

The 27th Donut Mystery.

Jessica Beck is the *New York Times* Bestselling Author of the
Donut Mysteries, the Classic Diner Mysteries, the Ghost
Cat Cozy Mysteries, and the Cast Iron Cooking Mysteries.

To P, forever and always,
For all the years, all the laughs, and all the love!

When an ice storm hits April Springs, it freezes more than the trees and power lines as one of the town's residents perishes outside. But soon Suzanne and Grace learn that it wasn't the cold that killed Santa-suit-wearing Greg Whitmore but a bullet instead. The women must do their best to figure out who killed the banker before someone else gets frozen out, permanently.

CHAPTER 1

THE CHARLOTTE TELEVISION STATIONS WERE all predicting the ice storm of the century for our part of North Carolina, but somehow the promised event felt more staged than real to me. I had a feeling that their scarily hyped warnings were more about the ratings than any actual dangerous weather pattern approaching us. After all, every year they issued at least one heavy-snow alarm for our area that usually offered only a flurry or two, so there was no reason to suspect that this ice-storm prediction was going to be any different.

It turned out that I was wrong about that, though: dead wrong.

When the storm finally hit April Springs—more than living up to all of the dire predictions—no one was more surprised than I was. Not only was the ice damage every bit as bad as they'd warned us to expect, but it ended up bringing something much worse with it.

One of the town's residents failed to make it through the storm, and the act left us all wondering what had brought Greg Whitmore to his bitter end.

One thing was certain; only time would tell.

"Now don't forget. I've got plenty of bail money if you need it," I told my husband as he packed his overnight travel bag.

"If things get dicey, I can be there in two hours to get you out of jail."

Jake laughed at my offer. "Suzanne, what exactly are you expecting might happen? It's a bachelor party for an old friend I served with when I was with the State Police. None of us are young men anymore, and I have a hunch it's going to be one of the tamest get-togethers anyone has ever witnessed. I still can't believe Lee is finally getting married. If ever there was a confirmed bachelor in my mind, he was it."

"I think it's sweet," I said as I slipped an extra pair of socks into his bag. Jake had a tendency to under-pack for every occasion, while I liked to be prepared for imagined situations that would leave even a Boy Scout ill equipped. "People can still hope to find love no matter how old they are. After all, just look at us."

My husband spotted the socks, started to toss them out, but then he must have thought better of it and put them back into his bag. "Suzanne, we're not *that* old," Jake said as he reached around and slapped my rear to prove it. "Besides, Lee is younger than me."

"I know, but he's not younger than *me*," I answered with a grin. "I suppose it's out of the question to invite myself along, isn't it?"

"Nobody else's spouses are coming," Jake said with a shrug, "but if you're worried about missing out on something, you're more than welcome to join me. I have a feeling we'll just sit around the fire at the lodge discussing old cases all weekend, the more gruesome the better."

"As tempting as you make it sound, I think I'll pass after all," I said. "Besides, Grace and I are going to have a sleepover here while you're gone. You're not worried about the weather, are you?" Every station in Charlotte had been predicting doom and gloom for us over the past three days, and it was starting to get to me.

"No worries on that front. If it does hit, it isn't supposed to be until later tonight, so we should all be at the lodge by then. We're not planning any field trips, and if I know Lee, there will be more than enough food and supplies to last us a month. If need be, but I'll be home for Christmas if I have to take a sled dog team."

"You don't really think the weather will be that bad, do you?" I asked him.

"I sincerely doubt it. Even if it's as rough as they say it's going to be, you and Grace should be fine here. There's plenty of firewood on the porch, so if you lose power, you won't be cold, and since the stove runs on natural gas, you won't go hungry, either. It's about as good a place to ride out an ice storm as I can imagine."

"Would it be selfish of me to say that I still wished you weren't going?" I asked him softly.

"No, and if it were for anyone else, I might try to beg off, but Lee saved my life once, and I'm not about to let him down now." Jake had recounted the tale to me one night long ago, how a very bad man had gotten behind him in a shootout, and only Lee's quick thinking and even quicker reactions had saved my husband's life. Jake had saved many more people himself over the years, but he took his core obligation to the groom very seriously.

"I get it. I really do," I said, suddenly feeling silly about how I'd been behaving. My husband had faced things much more dire than a storm in his life before we'd met, but I couldn't help being overprotective of him now that we were together. After all, it had taken me a great many years to find him, and I wasn't anywhere close to being ready to let him go. I went up on my tiptoes and kissed him soundly.

"What was that for?" he asked me with a grin after I pulled away.

"I want to give you the best reason I can to come back safely to me."

My sweet husband surprised me by lifting me up in his arms and twirling me around in the tight space of our bedroom. I laughed at the unexpected move, and we were both grinning when he finally put me back down. Somehow Jake had managed to break the tension without saying a word, and I loved him all the more for it. "Now, I'd better be on my way, just in case." He hesitated in the living room, where we'd set up a real Christmas tree this year and decorated it with ornaments from both our pasts. Sprigs of holly adorned the fireplace mantel, and there were shimmering garlands draped above the front door. Jake kissed me soundly one last time, and then we walked out onto the front porch together.

"Don't forget to call me when you get there," I reminded him as I took in the lovely, though quite chilly, day we were having. The sky was bright and blue and the December air crisp and clean, feeling freshly scrubbed as I drew in a deep breath. Surely they were wrong about our impending weather, just as they'd been wrong so many times in the past.

"I'll try, but I can't make any promises, since I may not be able to get a cell phone signal from the lodge, but I'll let you know when I pass through Boone," he said. "You stay warm and stay safe while I'm gone."

"Right back at you," I said, and then he drove away in my Jeep. Jake had wanted to take his old truck to the lodge, but I'd insisted that he drive my vehicle. It was designed for the kind of weather he might face, whereas I planned on staying home unless I positively, absolutely had to go somewhere. My donut shop was close by, just a short walk through the park, so I could easily make that on foot if I needed to. Jake had protested a little about taking my Jeep, but secretly, I thought he'd been glad that I'd insisted.

I hadn't planned on going anywhere myself when he left, but suddenly, I couldn't stand the thought of being in the cottage alone. I went back inside, grabbed my jacket and the keys to Jake's truck, and decided to go pay my mother a surprise visit. I hadn't spoken with her in three days, even though we lived so close, and I missed her. Driving through April Springs toward her place, it amazed me how the town had gone all out with its decorations. Our mayor and my good friend, George Morris, had yet another new secretary, a dynamo named Sue Boggs from Union Square. She'd spearheaded the decorating committee this year, and it had really paid off. Giant ornaments hung from the trees in the park, and each streetlight offered an oversized snowflake the size of a large pizza. Tinsel hung from every available surface, and a host of life-sized plastic Santas were scattered all over town, placed in the oddest spots and posed in some pretty hilarious positions. As I drove from my place to my mother's, I saw one who appeared to be trying to shimmy up the town clock across from city hall, one peering into an empty building on Springs Drive, and yet another perched on a bench in front of the hardware store supposedly reading a newspaper. Instead of the promised ice, I found myself wishing for snow to act as the perfect backdrop to all that the town had done to celebrate the season.

When I got to Momma's place, I found my stepfather poring over piles of old newspaper clippings at the kitchen table, but my mother was nowhere in sight. "Where's Momma?" I asked him as I walked right in, shedding my jacket along the way. The place was decorated for Christmas to the maximum extent, not only with a massive tree in place, fully decorated, but with a train set circling it, a wreath on the front door, and scattered decorations everywhere throughout the cozy space.

Phillip looked up and smiled at me, something that still took some getting used to. Phillip Martin had been our chief of police when I'd first started sleuthing, and we'd butted heads on more than one occasion, but now that he was retired, and married to my mother to boot, we'd managed to find not only a peaceful coexistence but almost a friendship as well.

"She went to the market, but she should be home soon. Are you stocked up for the storm?"

I realized there were a few things I might want in my pantry, since Grace was coming over. "I'm in pretty good shape, but I'll stop by on my way home to pick up a few odds and ends."

"If there's anything left by then," he answered with a grin. We both knew how storm-crazy our fellow townsfolk could get with anything more than a heavy frost predicted.

"What are you working on?" I asked him as I scanned the stacks of newspapers.

"I'm looking for another cold case to solve," he said with a frown.

"What candidates do you have so far?" I asked as I leaned over and looked at some of the top articles.

"Let's see, we've got two disappearances, three robberies, a hit and run, two homicides, and an honest-to-goodness holdup."

"Wow, all this happened in April Springs?" I asked, feeling myself being drawn into his hobby of investigating the coldest of cold cases, which had become a passion for him since he'd retired.

"In and around town, yes, but the oldest of these date back nearly a hundred years," he explained. "Take this case, for example. It happened over…"

At that moment, my momma walked in, her arms laden with groceries. "Phillip, don't bore the poor girl to death with your dusty old clippings," she said with a grin as she leaned over and kissed the top of his head.

"It's okay. I find it interesting," I said, coming to my stepfather's defense, something that still felt weird to be doing.

"Don't encourage him," she said with a smile as she started putting her groceries away. "Is Jake here with you?"

"No, why? Do I need to bring him with me every time I visit my own mother?" I asked her facetiously.

"Of course not. I just saw his truck parked out front, that's all."

"It's no big deal. I'm driving his truck for the next few days," I said. "How was the grocery store?"

"It is an absolute madhouse. How are your supplies?"

"They're fine," I said, "though I was just telling your husband that I might stop by for a treat or two."

"Is there anything here you'd like? You're welcome to whatever we have," she asked, offering me a pack of candy bars.

"Hey, those are mine," Phillip said with a grin, looking up long enough to see what she'd been offering me. "Not that I wouldn't mind splitting them with you, Suzanne."

"I got two packs," Momma said with a grin, "and all of the s'mores ingredients, too. I have a feeling tonight we're going to be happy we have a wood fireplace."

"Do you think it's really going to hit us?" I asked my mother.

"Probably not," she conceded, "but it's still a good excuse to have treats on hand. Now, why *exactly* are you driving your husband's truck?"

"Jake is on his way to a bachelor party in the mountains, so I let him have the Jeep," I explained. "After he left, I got a little lonely, so I thought I'd come by and see how you were doing."

"How very sweet. You know, you're more than welcome to stay here with us," Momma said. "It will be just like old times."

I didn't know what old times she was referring to, since I'd never stayed with the two of them since they'd married. I liked her husband well enough, but I wasn't in any hurry to stay there more than an hour or two at a time unless the circumstances were dire. It was nothing against them; I just liked having my own space.

Luckily, I had a readymade excuse that had the added benefit of being absolutely true. "Thanks, but Grace is coming over in a bit, and we're having a slumber party tonight."

"My, that sounds like fun," Momma said.

"You're welcome to join them if you'd like, Dot," Phillip said with a smile. "Goodness knows I've got plenty to keep myself busy here."

She patted his cheek warmly before she answered. "Thank you kindly for the offer, but truth be told, I'd rather be here with you when the lights go out." She smiled at me as she added, "No offense, Suzanne."

"None taken," I replied with a grin of my own. I never would have paired the two of them together, but somehow, they suited each other perfectly. It had been hard at first seeing my mother with anyone but my father, but I had to admit, she and Phillip made a happy couple. "Well, if things are as bad at the store as you say, I'd better get over there before they're out of everything."

"I could tag along and keep you company," Momma offered.

"Thanks, but I couldn't ask you to go through that gauntlet again just for my sake." I hugged her, feeling big and gawky and awkward as always as I towered over my own mother. She was a giant in every way but her stature, and it was easy to forget how petite she was, given her grand personality.

"Keep in touch throughout the evening, Suzanne," Momma said as she bundled up and walked me out to Jake's truck.

"You don't have to worry about me. I'll be fine," I said with a smile.

"Sorry, but it comes with the territory. There's no time that I *don't* worry about you," she replied, softening her statement with a pat on my shoulder. "It's a mother's prerogative."

"I'll talk to you later," I said, and then, over her shoulder, I said, "Good-bye, Phillip," who had left his work long enough to come out and say good-bye as well.

He waved a hand in my general direction and quickly ducked back inside, no doubt to dig into his stack of unsolved cases again.

Momma just laughed. "Be good."

"You know me. I'm always *very* good," I said with a laugh, and then I got into Jake's truck and headed for the grocery store. I had a feeling that it was going to be every bit as bad as Momma had related, but I still wasn't prepared for the madness I faced once I found a parking space for the truck and made my way inside.

CHAPTER 2

THE STORE HAD BEEN EVEN worse than I'd expected, and by the time I fought my way back outside, I realized that, all in all, it hadn't been worth the trouble. The bread, all of the bread, was long gone, and so was every kind of milk imaginable, including several different types of soy. The peanut butter was gone as well, and so were most of the jellies and jams. I'd ended up getting a bag of dry beans, two cans of whipped cream, and a pumpkin pie that had seen better days, its crust battered and beaten. On my way back home, I dropped by the donut shop to make sure that everything was safe and sound, and after that, it was time to head for the cottage and meet Grace. Her car was in her driveway as I drove by, and I thought about swinging in, but she'd be at my place soon enough, so I kept going.

She was there sooner than I'd expected, actually.

When I drove the truck into my driveway, I found Grace bundled up in a heavy coat as well as thick sporting gloves and a brightly knitted hat. She was sitting on the front porch swing, going back and forth and grinning like some kind of maniac.

"You walked over here?" I asked her as I got out and let her in the house.

"You'd better believe it. There's no way I'm risking my

company car in an ice storm. Besides, it's not *that* far." She spotted the bags and asked, "What did you get us?"

"It was slim pickings at the store," I said as I put my meager collection on the counter in the kitchen.

"Are you kidding? We've got pie! Everything else is icing on the cake."

"There's no icing for the pie, but I did manage to find two cans of whipped cream," I said.

"Brilliant. That way we won't have to fight over just one," she laughed. "Grab a couple of forks, and let's get started."

I did as she instructed, along with a knife for cutting the dessert treat. "Grace, are we seriously starting our evening out with pie?"

"What better way is there to do it?" she asked me with a grin.

I cut us both quarters of the small pie and put them on large plates.

"Good thinking," she said over my shoulder. "We want to leave plenty of room for the topping."

"I knew there was a reason you were my best friend," I said, laughing as I handed her plate to her, along with one of the cans.

It was the perfect way to start off our slumber party. I found myself wishing later that we hadn't had so many bad things happen so soon after. It was a shame to let the nice time we shared early on be forgotten in the aftermath that was to come.

After we finished our dinner, the pie first, of course, we were cleaning up as we discussed what we'd do next.

"I bought some movies today after I finished working in a territory with one of my reps," Grace said as she retrieved a few DVDs from her bag.

"What did you find?"

"Well, since the theme tonight is apparently going to be

ice, I bought *Ice Age*, *Frozen*, and one of the sequels to *Ice Age*. I thought about getting *The Ice Storm*, *Ice Station Zebra*, and *The Day After Tomorrow*, but I figured we could use some lighter fare, if things are going to get as intense as they're saying. What do you think?"

"Your selection sounds good to me," I said as the wind outside began to pick up and the sky started to darken quickly. The temperature had dropped several degrees in the past few hours, but I knew that it still wasn't cold enough in the upper atmosphere for the snow I'd rather be getting. I was a bit of a weather nerd as a kid, and I'd done my junior high science fair project on the different forms of precipitation, so I knew that for freezing rain to occur, the upper atmosphere temperature had to be above freezing, while the temperature on the ground had to be below it. The icy rain, still liquid, hit the frozen surfaces below and froze instantly, coating the world in its icy embrace. As the wind blew harder and harder, I could hear tapping on the glass outside, and when I looked out, I saw that there was some sleet mixing in with the freezing rain. "It's getting started earlier than I thought it would," I told Grace.

She looked outside and shivered a little. "Do you think the forecasters finally got one right?"

"Maybe," I said. "I hope Jake is okay."

"You should call him."

"I don't like to pester him when he's driving," I answered.

"Suit yourself, but if it were me, I'd call him in a heartbeat."

It didn't take much for her to persuade me. I dialed Jake's number, fully expecting to get his voicemail, when he surprised me by picking up on the third ring instead. "Hey. I was going to call you in a few minutes. How's it going?"

"The bad weather is just starting here," I reported. "How about you?"

"The skies are gray, but that doesn't mean a thing. I left Boone ten minutes ago, so I should be at the lodge in about half an hour. I've been warned to expect to lose my signal pretty soon, though. Is Grace there with you?"

"She is. We had pie for dinner, and potato soup for dessert," I said.

"Hi, Jake," Grace said loudly, laughing as she did.

"Don't have too much fun without me, you hear?" he asked.

"Sorry, but it's too late for that," I said, happy to hear his voice, even if he'd be out of range soon. The mountains could be that way, yielding a clear signal one second and then a dozen feet down the road not letting us pick anything up at all. "Have fun."

"You, too," he said, and then the signal dropped out entirely, and he was gone.

I put my phone aside with a shrug. "I'm glad I called. Thanks for the advice. Now, let's do the dishes and then start that first movie."

As we watched the first film, the howling wind picked up outside, but the pelting against the glass stopped. I knew that wasn't a good thing. The rain was freezing on contact now instead of in the air, and that was how an ice storm was born. Sure enough, I looked out the window again and saw that the glass was starting to get a fine glaze on it. The lights in the park were all wearing the beginnings of icy beards, and I wondered how long we'd have power.

An hour later, my question was answered. There was a loud explosion, followed quickly by the sound of something crashing to the ground, and then the lights were suddenly extinguished, killing our movie as well.

With no power in the cottage, the only heat we had now was from the fireplace, so it was natural enough for us to sleep out on the couches in the living room where the warmth was. We each bundled up and chatted about the things best friends talk about, and soon enough, I found myself drifting off to sleep, warm and full.

I hoped my fellow townsfolk were faring a tenth as well as Grace and I were.

Only one of them didn't make it through to the other side of the storm.

The phone rang in the middle of the night, and I was surprised to be getting a call from anyone at that hour. Grace didn't even move as I answered.

"Hello?" I asked softly.

"Suzanne, we're not working today, are we?" my assistant Emma Blake asked me.

I peeked outside and saw that the night was still blanketed in darkness. "I'm afraid not. Without power, we won't be able to do anything, so there's no use going in. Go back to sleep."

"This storm is crazy, isn't it?" she asked me excitedly.

"Crazy enough. Are you all doing okay?"

"Mom and Dad are gone to the world, but I can't seem to sleep when I know I should be at the donut shop, no matter what the circumstances might be."

"Sorry about that. You've got the same curse I do," I told her softly.

"What's that?"

"You're too conscientious."

"No. That can't be it," she said with a laugh.

"I'll talk to you later, Emma. Thanks for calling."

I threw a few more logs on the fire, and then I settled back onto the couch. I fell asleep almost immediately, and even the shotgun explosions of tree limbs breaking free in the darkness weren't enough to keep me awake.

CHAPTER 3

N O SURPRISE, I WOKE UP before Grace did, and I felt chilled from the lower temperature of the cottage. The fireplace held only coals, but there were enough there still glowing to generate real flames not long after I added some dry wood to the embers. Once I had that going and the room started to get toasty again, I set about making us breakfast. There would be no donuts today, not without power at Donut Hearts, but that didn't mean that we had to skip breakfast. I snuck into the kitchen and whipped us up some pumpkin pancakes, Grace's new favorite. Before the first pancake was off the griddle perched on my gas stovetop, my best friend joined me. "You made breakfast?" she asked me with a smile as she rubbed her eyes.

"Your favorite," I said. "How do you manage to look so good crawling out of bed first thing in the morning?"

She grinned at me. "I'd like to say that it's due to clean living and healthy eating, but really, it's just a matter of good genes. I'd take credit for it if I could, but since I can't, I won't."

I slid a pancake onto her plate. "Dig in."

"Have you already eaten?" she asked me as she started to take her first bite.

"No, the cook eats last. It's one of the rules that I often love to break."

Grace took another bite, smiled as she swallowed it, and

then laughed. "If *I* were cooking, there would be a brand-new set of rules."

"Don't worry about me. I'm having the next one," I said. "Did you hear all of the commotion outside last night?"

"No, I slept like the dead," she answered, an unfortunate expression but one she used every now and then. "Why? Did I miss something?"

"Just the ice storm," I said. "I take it Emma's phone call didn't wake you in the middle of the night."

"No, I never heard it, either. Why, did she want to come in to work this morning?"

"She did. So did I, as a matter of fact, but without power, I knew that there was no use even going over to Donut Hearts. After we eat, would you like to trek over there with me through the park? I want to make sure nothing happened to the building in the night."

"Sure, I'm game if you are," she said as I slid the next pancake onto my plate. "We don't have to go just yet though, do we?"

I had to laugh at the not-so-subtle hint. "No, I'm sure there's enough time for another pancake."

"Or maybe even two," she answered with a smile.

Once we'd finished eating, I put the dishes in the sink, since I wasn't about to wash them in cold water. The stove was gas, but my water heater was electric, something I meant to correct if I ever had enough of a windfall to convert it over. We both bundled up in warm clothes, and Grace borrowed an extra scarf of mine my mother had picked up for me on one of her trips to Ireland a few years earlier. That was always her gift to me when she visited there, and I had half a dozen of the best scarves money could buy. I chose one for myself to complete my ensemble, we put on our boots and heavy jackets, and then we stepped outside.

It was breathtaking, even though I knew how potentially

deadly the ice storm had been. It had passed us by now though, and the sun was shining brightly as everything around us seemed to be coated in fine diamonds.

"Man oh man, it's cold," Grace said as she pulled the scarf closer.

"I know, but isn't it gorgeous?" I asked her as I looked around in wonder. Though I knew the storm could prove fatal for some, there was no denying the beauty it left behind in its wake. Branches, and even entire trees, were covered with nearly half an inch of ice, as though they had been encased in glass. The downside to that was that there were several large branches lying on the ground as well. The trees hadn't been able to support them, given the added weight of the ice. The grass crunched under our feet as we walked in the park, and I spotted the downed power line near the Boxcar Grill before Grace did. "Careful," I said as I gave it a wide berth.

"You don't have to tell me," she said as she neatly sidestepped it. "Wow, it's amazing how much damage a little ice can do, isn't it?"

"I can't even imagine how slick the roads must be," I said. "Nobody's driving anywhere anytime soon, or at least until it melts."

"Which shouldn't take too long, given the way the sun is shining and the temperature is starting to warm up," Grace added as she turned her face up to the warmth. "The limbs are already dripping from moisture, and I have a hunch it won't be long before life gets back to normal around here. Have you heard from Jake today?"

"No, but I imagine where he is, he just got snow."

"I kind of envy him that," Grace said as she nodded. "I wouldn't mind having a white Christmas."

"This is probably as close as we're going to get to it," I said as I noticed one of the mayor's plastic snowmen sitting on one of the park benches between my cottage, the Boxcar Grill, and Donut Hearts.

Grace noticed it at the same time I did. "I think George is getting a little carried away with those things, don't you? I saw one yesterday that looked as though it were about to steal a car."

"I think they're fun," I said, but as we got closer, I realized that there was nothing fun about this one.

The second I realized what I was seeing, I pulled out my cell phone and dialed 911.

"What's going on, Suzanne?" Grace asked me.

"That's not a plastic Santa," I said as I was connected with the police station.

At least my cell phone was working.

I wouldn't have wanted to walk up the icy sidewalk to get help.

I told the cop on phone duty, "This is Suzanne Hart. Grace Gauge and I are out walking in the park, and we just found a man in a Santa suit frozen to death on one of the benches near the Boxcar Grill."

"Are you sure he's dead?" the dispatcher asked me.

"Yes, Darby, I'm sure," I told the cop on the other end. I looked at the clearly frozen man sitting there and tried to figure out who it was. It was hard to tell though, since his face was nearly completely covered by an icy white beard. What skin I could see was pale white though, and a layer of ice covered his eyes and nose, at least from what I could see from where I was standing. Was it possible it was Phillip, my stepfather, under the beard? This man matched his size and stature, and I worried for one split second that this could be a blow my mother would never recover from, but then I looked around the eyes, and I knew that it wasn't him.

That still didn't explain who it was, though.

"There's no need to get testy with me, Suzanne. None of us have gotten a wink of sleep because of the storm. We'll be over there as soon as we can make it. You just need to calm down and not get upset."

I sympathized with him, but I had problems of my own. "How long will that be, Darby? Are we talking minutes? Hours? Days?" The last thing I wanted to hear was someone telling me not to get upset. Did that ever work on *anyone?*

"Minutes," he said, and then he hung up on me.

"Someone's on his way, sometime today," I told Grace as I started taking photographs of the man on the bench with my cell phone. It was more a matter of habit than anything else, but I wanted to document what Grace and I had just found, as though it would help me somehow come to grips with it. My best friend pulled her own cell phone out and started to dial it as well. "Who are you calling?" I asked her.

"No worries, Suzanne. We won't have long to wait. Stephen will handle this," she said. Her boyfriend was the chief of police, so he probably would try to make an appearance faster.

I wasn't sure it was the right thing to do, though. "Grace, he's got his hands full, what with this storm and all. Let's just wait until Darby can send someone."

She frowned for a moment, and then she shrugged as she put away her phone. "Okay."

"It shouldn't be long," I said, and then I glanced over at my donut shop.

My heart fell when I saw that a large tree had toppled across the road and had landed squarely on my lovely building.

It appeared the storm had done more damage than I'd first suspected.

It wasn't another fatality, but it almost felt like one.

CHAPTER 4

"**G**RACE, WOULD YOU MIND WAITING here for the police without me? I need to see what's going on at my shop."

"Suzanne, there's no reason either one of us should stay here. Clearly we can't help this poor guy. When the cops show up, we'll point them in this general direction, but for now, I'm coming with you."

As soon as she said it, I knew that she was right. Whoever this man was, there was nothing we could do for him, and I needed to see the extent of the damage Donut Hearts had suffered during the storm. I had insurance on the business, but it wasn't very good, and I wasn't sure how much of the storm damage it would cover. Jake and I weren't exactly rolling in spare cash, but I knew in a pinch, I could always borrow from Momma and pay her back in installments. I'd have to worry about that later, though. Right now I had to get in there, assess the damage, and see what it would take to make things right again.

If someone had asked me the day before, I would have said that there was no way the tree that was now sitting partially in my donut shop could have ever reached it from where it had stood for over a hundred years in the park. It had been a direct hit, but at least it hadn't been closer.

It was bad enough as it was.

The top branches had crashed into the shop, shattering my front window and damaging some of the bricks that made up the front and left side exterior walls. I could easily see inside without going through the front door, something that was pretty alarming to view. As Grace and I stood there, the tree shifted a little, and I found my best friend tugging at my arm. "Suzanne, we can't go in there. It's not safe."

"It will be fine," I said as I pulled against her grip, trying to release it.

"Of course it will, because we're both staying right here until we can get someone to help us deal with this."

She pulled out her cell phone, and I said, "Grace, I told you before. We can't call the police chief."

"I'm not calling Stephen," she said with a grin. "I'm going even higher up the chain of command."

"You're phoning the mayor?" I asked, knowing that George Morris had to have his hands full as well.

"I'm going even higher than that. I'm calling your mother. If anyone can get us some help over here on the double, she's the one."

I knew that Grace was right, and I probably should have thought of it myself, but I was still in shock, not only from the damage to my shop, but more importantly, finding the man sitting across the street who'd lost his life in the ice storm. "Hand me the phone," I said. "I'll talk to her."

"You're going to ask her for help, aren't you? I shouldn't have to remind you that this is no time to be stubborn."

"I can't afford to be stubborn at the moment." When she picked up, I said, "Momma, I need your help."

"Are you all right, child?" she asked.

"I'm fine, but the donut shop got hit by a falling tree during the storm."

Momma didn't even miss a beat as she took in the news. "Are you there right now?"

"Grace and I are standing outside," I said, not mentioning

the body we'd just found in the park. There would be time for that later.

"Don't go in. I'll have a crew there in ten minutes."

"How can you promise that?" I asked her. The streets were quickly absorbing heat from the sun, and most of the ice was now beginning to puddle, but I couldn't imagine having that kind of pull with anyone.

"Don't you worry about that. I'm just glad you're okay."

"Did you two survive the storm all right?" I asked her, remembering how I'd felt when I thought it might have been Phillip we'd found earlier.

"No worries on that count. We're both fine," she said. After a closer examination, I'd known that it hadn't been her husband dead on that park bench, but I still felt a wave of relief having it confirmed. "Now let me get off the line so I can get busy."

"Thanks, Momma."

"It's my pleasure," she said. "Be sure to take plenty of pictures. You'll need them for the insurance company."

I hadn't even thought about that. "That's good advice."

"That's what a mother is for," she said, and then she was gone.

Ninety seconds later, a squad car pulled up in front of us. It was good to see that it could maneuver on the wet pavement. I'd done as my mother had suggested, and I'd taken a few dozen photos of the building with my phone. After calling my insurance agent, I was assured that as long as I documented everything, we should be fine. The poor man was up to his eyebrows in repair estimates, but Momma had known him for thirty years, so there was a level of trust there that went far beyond what he might have had with a regular client. Besides, I had a hunch that my mother's business with her many properties kept him highly profitable, so that surely helped as well.

Chief Grant got out, looked at the donut shop, and whistled softly to himself. "I'm so sorry that happened, Suzanne."

"It's being dealt with," I said. "The man we called about is over there."

The police chief nodded, smiled at Grace for a second, and then he told us both, "I'll see you two in a few minutes. Don't go inside the donut shop, no matter how tempted you might be to go in and look around."

"We weren't about to," I said, maybe a little too testily. Softening my tone of voice, I continued. "Sorry. I'm a little on edge. Momma's mobilizing a crew even as we speak."

"Then I'm sure that you're in good hands," he said, and then the chief walked over to the bench where we'd found the frozen man, still sitting up and staring at exactly nothing.

"Who do you suppose it is?" Grace asked me as we watched Stephen approach the body.

"I have no idea, but I'm sure we'll find out soon enough. These storms can be really scary, can't they?"

"I thought it was fun last night, but this morning it's lost a lot of its joy for me," she admitted. Grace must have realized how she'd sounded, because she quickly added, "You mustn't worry. I'm sure Donut Hearts will be fine."

"I hope you're right," I said. As we stood there, two other police cars arrived, along with an ambulance. "I wonder if they'll be able to thaw him out enough to get him on the gurney?" I asked her.

"I don't even want to think about that," Grace answered, shivering for a moment, but not from the chill still in the air. "Wow, I don't know how she did it, but your mother came through in aces. Here comes the cavalry."

I looked down Springs Drive and saw that Grace was right. Barreling toward us was a large truck from a tree-removal service in Maple Hollow, followed by two smaller work trucks that had been bashed and battered over the years.

"Which one of you is Ms. Hart?" a burly-looking man asked us as he got out of the big truck.

"I am," I said. "I'd offer you donuts while you work, but I'm afraid I won't be able to do that today."

He grinned at me. "No worries, ma'am. We've been up working since four a.m., so we're all set. We'll have this taken care of in no time."

"I really appreciate you coming out on such short notice," I said.

"Thank your mother. The woman is difficult to say no to, isn't she?"

"Tell me about it," I answered with a smile. "Try growing up as her kid."

"Thanks, but no thanks," he replied with a grin.

The team was as good as the man's word, working quickly and efficiently in taking care of the segment of tree that had battered my shop, separating the part that had fallen on my land from the balance of the tree that was still blocking the road. Once the main branches were removed, I could see that a small section of the front left corner walls and the roof were both on the floor, which was also littered with shards of glass from the broken front window. It made me sick to my stomach to see my beloved donut shop in such a state of disrepair.

"Boss, should we take care of the part of the tree that's still in the road?" one of the young men asked him.

"Well, she's not going to be able to get anyone else in here until we do, now is she? Let's go, guys. We need to be back in Maple Hollow in thirty minutes, so hustle."

They cut up the log breaching the road and moved the larger pieces with a boom arm on the back of their truck, stacking it all neatly beside the pavement. "The city will take care of the rest," he said as the last of the branches went into the wood chipper. The machine made a sudden grinding noise every time a new branch went in, and I felt myself flinching a little as the wood was instantly turned into chips.

They'd even started to sweep up when I interceded. "That's fine. Do I pay you now, or will you bill me later?"

"It's already been taken care of. Have a nice day, ma'am."

"You, too," I said. "Sorry for the extra work."

He laughed. "Don't be. Our kids are going to have some pretty wonderful Christmases with all of the overtime work we're getting." Then his smile died as they rolled the body to the ambulance. At least they'd been able to get the faux Santa strapped in and lying prone. "That's a real shame, isn't it? The homeless don't have a chance in this kind of weather."

Was he homeless, though? That Santa suit hadn't been poor quality. Someone had spent good money on it. I decided not to point that out, though. "Thanks again."

"Happy to help," he said a little more somberly. "Let's go, guys. We're burning daylight."

After they were gone, I had a better chance to assess the damage to the donut shop, and what I found there was almost overwhelming. I knew somehow, I'd get through it. What pained me the most was not being able to call Jake and tell him all that had happened. I had a feeling he was snowed in where he was in the mountains, and I wouldn't see him for several days, despite the fact that he had my Jeep.

As things stood, I knew that I'd just have to soldier on without him.

CHAPTER 5

I T WAS A REAL MESS.

I wasn't sure what I'd been expecting to see once the tree had been removed completely, but seeing the raw damage was something else entirely. A good portion of the front left corner of the building, made up of a combination of brick and wood, was on the floor of the shop, along with a section of roof. My couches and chairs where my customers sat and enjoyed their donuts and coffee were ruined. The concrete floor, painted long ago in a plum tone, was wrecked as well, chipped in several places and scratched in quite a few more. The tables and chairs out front had been destroyed as well, and the awning was in a heap on the ground near the front door.

The good news? The glass display cases where we displayed our donuts were miraculously unscathed; nothing bad had happened in the kitchen that couldn't be fixed; and Emma and I were alive. If that tree had hit while we'd been open for business, I hated to think of what might have happened to any customers who'd have been unlucky enough to be in my shop. I decided to focus on the fact that Donut Hearts had been empty and be happy that no matter what the rest of the day might bring, I could still call the day a success.

The tree-service folks had been gone all of two minutes when I heard horns honking outside. The street noise was incredible, which I should have expected, given the fact that my donut shop had been torn open like a lemon-filled pastry. I looked out through the opening that had once housed my front window to see George Morris in his truck, along with folks in four other vehicles. The mayor pulled up right in front of the shop, while the others scattered their cars along the drive and joined him.

"What's going on?" I asked him, bewildered by the sudden activity.

"We're your work crew," George said with a grin. "Your mother called me."

"I really wish she hadn't," I said. I didn't mind her calling in favors from people who were paid for their labors, but these people were all my friends. I noticed several good customers among the group and shared their condolences for what had happened.

"We're happy to be here," the mayor said. "Don't worry. We'll have you fixed up in no time."

I looked at my damaged building. "No offense, but I don't see how that's possible."

"Oh, it won't be as good as new, but it should hold you until you can get some real craftsmen in here to fix the place up. We've got plywood, timber, nails, roofing paper, and some Plexiglas. You'll be set before you know it."

"I don't know what to say," I replied, nearly choked with tears over the kindness of my friends. I was certain they had their own problems to deal with because of the ice storm, but they'd put them all aside to pitch in and help me get back on my feet.

"Just say thank you, and we can move on," the mayor said happily. Disaster relief was clearly one of the bright spots of his job, not that I minded.

"Thank you," I said loudly. "When I get going again, there will be donuts for everyone, on the house."

There was a loud cheer from the group, and then George took over. "Sam, Jim, Bobby, let's get that furniture loaded in the panel vans. You can take everything over to the city hall basement to dry out. Gina, Tom, Vince, Carl, let's get started on framing up some temporary walls so we can put on a new section of roof. Don't worry about it being sexy; it just has to keep everything inside safe and dry."

"What should Grace and I do?" I asked the mayor as I watched everyone getting busy.

"Unless I miss my guess, you're going to be busy in a few minutes yourself."

"Doing what?"

He nodded to a man I hadn't noticed before down the street, and suddenly, the power came back on as the emergency lights flickered in the donut shop and then came on. "Making donuts for the work crews," he said with a smile. "You're going to have a chance to make good on your offer this morning."

"Nothing would make me happier."

"I'll help, too," Grace said as Momma, Phillip, Emma, and Sharon showed up. "We're here to be a part of the donut brigade," Momma said after she hugged me. In a soft voice, she whispered in my ear, "I'm covering your expenses today, so don't worry about what anything costs. We need to make donuts for the entire town, on the house. Everyone's digging out, and your goodies will lighten a great many spirits. What do you say? You supply the labor, I supply the materials, and we'll have crews deliver the goodies for us. Is it a deal?"

"It is," I said, hugging her briefly before I started sobbing. "You are amazing."

"I take after my daughter," she said, and I'd never been prouder of her than I was at that moment.

Grace said, "Not that I'm not willing to help you make donuts all morning, but why don't I organize things out here? I'll get folks to deliver the donuts you make. I always was better at logistics."

"That sounds like a plan to me," I said as I hugged her too. I was going to have to stop hugging people, or I was never going to get anything done.

Emma, Sharon, and I walked back into the kitchen. I flipped on the fryer and started mixing up batter for our cake donuts. There wouldn't be any yeast offerings today. Not only were they quite a bit fussier, but they took longer to make as well. Today, quick and dirty was going to be the order of the day.

After that, it was all a blur. The moment we'd made four dozen iced cake donuts, we started getting into the spirit of things as Emma, Sharon, and I started whipping out a wide range of donuts using banana, orange, Kool-Aid, pumpkin, and anything else we had on hand.

After two hours of solid donut making, I turned the reins over to Emma and Sharon to see what kind of progress they were making out front. I'd heard a great deal of hammering during the entire time that I'd been working, but I had no idea if they'd made much progress at all.

What I found there simply amazed me.

Temporary walls were now in place, covered with light-shaded sheets of plywood on the outside. Not only had they buttoned up the corner of the building, but they'd also done a nice job rough-framing the roof, and knowing George, they'd probably already sheathed it with tarpaper as well. A large piece of Plexiglas now covered the opening where the window had once been. It was incredible what they'd managed to do in such a short time. Several people were standing around eating donuts and drinking coffee as I walked out, and George grinned as I approached him.

"We aren't loitering. We just finished up. It's not glamorous by any stretch of the imagination, but it should hold you until you can get it fixed right. There's tar paper on the roof, so rain won't be an issue." He looked at the battered floor and shook his head. "Sorry, we couldn't do anything about that. You'll have to get that seen to as well."

"You want to know something? I've been thinking about changing the color anyway," I said with a smile. "I'm in the mood for something not plum, if you know what I mean. This is magnificent."

"So are your donuts," the mayor said. "There are four crews running them all over town. How long can you folks keep it up back there?"

I thought about the supplies we had on hand, did a quick calculation in my head, and then answered. "We can make about a hundred dozen more before we start running out of flour. That's the main thing. Should we keep at it?"

"If you wouldn't mind," he said. "Listen, we'll try to help you cover your losses today, one way or another."

"No worries, Mr. Mayor," I said with a smile. "Momma's already taken care of it."

"That woman is a saint," he said.

"Sure. Why not? She's a saint," I said with a laugh. I knew, better than anyone, that my mother had some excellent qualities, but I never would have used the word "saint" to describe her, and that was to her credit, in my mind.

"You know what I mean," George said, realizing the magnitude of what he'd just said. "I don't even have to feel bad about eating another one of these now," he said as he snagged a blueberry donut from the tray on the counter.

"Wow, you really are living on the edge," I said. "Usually you're an unglazed cake man."

"What can I say? Today is the day to live dangerously. At least your front door is still intact, so you'll be able to lock the place up when you leave this afternoon."

"Any word on the man we found in the park?" I asked him quietly, taking the conversation in a more serious direction.

"Haven't you heard?" he asked me.

"How could I have heard anything? I've been locked up in back making donuts all morning."

"It was Greg Whitmore," the mayor said sadly.

"Greg wasn't homeless," I said, remembering what the tree man had said earlier.

George looked startled by my statement. "I never said that he was."

"My point is, why was he out in the freezing rain when he had a nice safe home to go to?"

"I have no idea, but I'm sure we'll find out sooner or later. In the meantime, there's a town to put back together now that we're finished here."

"How bad was the storm in general?" I asked him.

"Not too awful. We're going to replace a few more windows with Plexiglas, patch a few more roofs, and then we'll be ready to start cutting up downed trees. The power is mostly restored here in town, and crews are working on the town's outer limits even as we speak. All in all, it could have been a great deal worse than it was."

"If you weren't Greg Whitmore," I added.

"Yes, indeed," the mayor said somberly, and then he dismissed the sadness as he brushed a few crumbs off his face. "Now, if you'll excuse us, we have to get cracking."

"Send anyone you find who's hungry our way, and we'll feed them," I said. "We'll have donuts and coffee to last at least until one."

"You're my kind of people, Suzanne."

"That's good, because I'm kind of fond of you myself." A little louder, I said, "Thank you, everyone. Your hard work and your willingness to help me won't be forgotten."

Carl Hancock looked at me and grinned. "Enough to get us free coffee and donuts for life?"

Everyone laughed, and when it died down, I said, "No, I could never afford to feed you that much," I said as I patted his portly belly.

He blushed a little, so I walked over and picked up a Kool-Aid donut and handed it to him. "But for today, it's an all-you-can-eat buffet."

"I'll take whatever I can get," he said with a smile before he took a big bite of the donut.

Ten minutes later, the floor was swept, the leftover pieces of wood had all been removed, and someone had brought a dozen folding chairs to the shop on loan from the fire department. That was just one of the reasons I knew I would never leave April Springs. It was too much like one big family.

I knew the glow I was feeling at the moment wouldn't last forever, but I expected it to linger longer than it did. Ten minutes after the construction and cleaning crew left Donut Hearts for other parts of town, the chief of police walked into the shop, and from the dour look on his face, it was immediately obvious that he wasn't there for the free donuts.

CHAPTER 6

"I've got an ID on the body you found," he told me.

"It was Greg Whitmore," I said.

"Who told you that, Suzanne?" the police chief asked, looking slightly vexed that I'd gotten the news somewhere else first.

"George Morris just left," I said. "Did Greg die from exposure?"

"No," the chief said.

That was news to me. "Was it a heart attack? I saw his face, Chief. It was covered in ice. How did he not die from the elements?"

"The truth of the matter was that he was dead before the cold could get him," Chief Grant said, lowering his voice. "I don't want the word to get out yet, but when I told Grace a few minutes ago, she insisted that I clue you in as well."

"If it wasn't the ice storm, then what was it?"

"A small-caliber bullet to the back of the head," the chief said as he shook his head in disgust.

"What?" I asked, much louder than I needed to. "I didn't see a bullet wound."

"Suzanne, could you keep your voice down? I don't want anyone in the kitchen to hear this."

"Sorry," I said, modulating my tone to a softer level. "Are you sure?"

"The coroner's pretty certain, what with the entry wound

coupled with the bullet he pulled out of Greg's head," the chief said. "Don't blame yourself for not spotting it. The EMTs missed it, too, and they were a lot closer to him than you were."

"So, somebody waited until he was sitting alone on a park bench, and they decided to shoot him in the middle of an ice storm?"

"Think about it. There were a lot of branches snapping off last night in the storm," the police chief said with a shrug. "How easy would it have been to mistake a gunshot for a branch breaking?"

"Pretty easy," I said, remembering how the sound had reminded me of gunfire the night before.

"That's what I think," the chief said. "Whoever did it had to have gotten pretty close to him. There were powder burns on his neck, but after he was dead, someone pulled the hat down so you couldn't see it."

"Who would want to kill Greg Whitmore?" I asked Chief Grant. Greg was a customer of mine at the donut shop, and I knew that he'd had more than his fair share of hard times, but to be murdered like that? I couldn't fathom it.

"That's what I'm aiming to find out," the police chief said. "I don't suppose there's any use telling you not to look into this yourself, is there?"

"That depends. What did Grace say when you asked her that question?"

He shook his head and grinned despite the way he must have felt. "What do you *think* she said? Just try to stay out of my way, Suzanne. I'm having a hard enough time as it is explaining to some folks around town why you keep getting mixed up in murder."

"Chief, to be fair, I usually don't go looking for it, but come on. Grace and I found the body, and I've known Greg for a long time. Did you really think I'd back off?"

"No, but I can always hope, can't I?" he asked. "Anyway, I thought you should know."

"Have you spoken to Lori?"

"His wife? Yeah, we've chatted a bit, but I'm nowhere near finished with her. It turns out that she was his soon-to-be ex-wife, did you know that? Turns out they were splitting up."

I remembered the time Lori had come by the donut shop when Greg had been released from the hospital, and she'd bought out my remaining inventory, since her husband had been craving my treats while he'd been in. She'd seemed so much in love with the man then. I wondered what had happened to them. I knew it happened that way sometimes, one person in a marriage no longer wanted to try, seemingly out of the blue, but it was never easy for the jilted spouse to come to terms with it. "I had no idea. Was anyone else involved?"

"Are you asking me if Greg was seeing another woman?"

"Or Lori might have been with another man," I clarified.

"I don't know yet, but I will. Listen, I don't mind you digging into Greg's life as long as you stay away from my official police investigation, but if you find anything out, and I mean anything, you come to me. Is that understood?"

"Loud and clear," I said. "Thanks for letting us do this."

The police chief grinned for a moment, and I saw the young man and not the policeman. "Did I really have any choice?"

"If it helps you sleep at night believing it, then why not?"

"Anyway, Grace thought you should know." He spotted the basket of donuts on the counter and the urn of coffee beside it. "Are those for anybody?"

"You more than most," I said with a grin. "Help yourself. Today it's all on the house. I even got the mayor to take a free donut and cup of coffee."

"That's just about too hard to believe," Stephen Grant said as he helped himself. "At least let me leave you a tip."

"That's your call entirely, but it's not expected, at least not today."

He slid a buck into the jar, and I realized that I should probably empty it, as it was nearly overflowing from the generosity of my fellow townsfolk. They'd come out in force, showing me with their labor as well as their wallets how much they cared for me. It was enough to make me cry again, but I'd vowed that I'd shed enough tears to last me the rest of the year, and some of the next one as well.

The moment Chief Grant was gone, I pulled out my cell phone and called Grace. "Hey, I just heard the news."

"About Greg? It's terrible, isn't it? I didn't recognize him, did you?"

"No, I didn't have a clue. Chief Grant just came by to tell me, so thanks for that. Apparently we have his provisional approval to dig into Greg Whitmore's murder."

"I'm the one who twisted his arm, remember?" Grace asked. "I thought I'd come by and we could get started. What do you think?"

I looked at the donuts we had left and did a quick calculation in my mind. "Give me an hour, and I'll be free and clear here," I said. "Now that I can lock the place up, I'll be able to leave it with a clear conscience."

"I can't remember the last time I had a clear conscience about anything," Grace said with a giggle, and then she hung up.

There was a part of me that wished we could get started right away, but I wasn't going anywhere until the last donut was handed out and the last drop of coffee was drained. The folks of April Springs had come out to help me, and I was going to make sure that I gave them everything I had back in return.

That reminded me. I had something I had to take care of immediately. I called Melissa Henderson, my flour supplier, and got her voicemail. "Hey, Melissa, it's Suzanne in April Springs. Call me when you get this."

I'd no sooner ended the call and put my cell phone away than it started ringing. It was Melissa, and she sounded as though she were out of breath. "Sorry about that," she said, panting a little. "My best friend lost her power, so we're having a big cookout. We're grilling steaks, chicken, and hamburgers, so if you're hungry and you can get to Maple Hollow, you're more than welcome to join us."

"You know, you *could* just put everything outside in the cold," I suggested. "You don't need electricity to keep things chilled in an ice storm. They'll probably save just fine being stored outside until the power gets turned back on."

"Now why on earth would we want to do that? We're making it a block party, Suzanne. It's as good an excuse as any to get together. You said on the phone that you needed flour?"

"I'm completely out," I said. "Baking powder, baking soda, yeast, too; all of it. How soon can you get me new supplies?"

"The roads should be clear by now. Will someone be around?"

"I'm not sure. Tell your driver I'll leave the front door unlocked in case no one is here."

"Is that wise?" she asked me.

"Honestly, there's not much left worth stealing, so I feel pretty good about taking my chances. They can lock up when they leave."

"Can do," she said. "Don't forget, it's an open invitation. Bring Jake, if you'd like."

"I'm tempted, but he's in the mountains north of Boone," I said.

"Then he got hit with snow. It's better than ice though, isn't it?"

"In more ways than I can imagine," I told her.

"Melissa, let's go. Everybody's getting hungry," I heard someone tell her on the other end of the line.

"I'm coming, Sandy," she said. "Sorry, I've got to go. Don't worry about your order. You'll be all set in no time."

"I appreciate that," I said. "Have a good party."

"You know it," Melissa said, and then we ended the call. She wasn't just my supplier; she'd become my dear friend over the years. Honestly, if I hadn't had Greg's murder to investigate, I would have been tempted to close the donut shop then and there and drive straight to Maple Hollow. After all, it really did sound like a fun party. I decided to call two other suppliers so I'd be set on coffee and the other necessities I had in my world, and fortunately, they were all able to deliver sooner than Melissa's operator could.

It turned out that I ended up being glad that I'd stuck around though, when a stranger walked through the front door of the donut shop twenty minutes before I had planned on closing, and by the look on his face, he had something he really needed to say.

CHAPTER 7

"**A**RE YOU SUZANNE HART?" AN older man with a trim frame and wire-rim glasses perched on his nose asked me.

Rarely was that ever good news for me, at least in my experience. "Maybe I am, maybe I'm not," I said with a shrug.

He grinned at me. "Relax, I'm not a process server. I've got a message for you from Jake."

"I'm Suzanne, then," I said hurriedly. "Have you heard from him? Why is he calling you and not me? Is he hurt? Did something happen to him?"

The words spilled out of me as I worried that something might have happened to my husband. A thousand nightmare scenarios played out in my mind in the instant it took him to answer. "He's fine," the man assured me. "My name's Kelly Bridges, ma'am. I'm a ham radio operator, and somebody got in touch with me from the lodge where he's staying. He sends his love and said for you to keep warm." The man frowned for a moment before he added, "Oh, there's one more thing. I hope this makes more sense to you than it did to me. He said to tell you that it turns out he's not going to need the bail money after all, whatever that means."

"It means, my good man, that you get a donut and a cup of coffee on the house for delivering his message," I said. "Shoot, I'm feeling especially generous today. Why don't you have two."

He patted his trim belly and grinned. "I don't mind if I do. Ma'am, I hate to be nosy, but is your husband in trouble?"

"What, are you asking me about the bail? No, it's just a joke we have between us."

The man held up his free hand and grinned. "No need to explain, then. The missus and I have a thousand little inside jokes between us, too. It drives our daughter absolutely crazy, which is part of the fun of it. From what I gathered, he'll be there for a few days before they can dig their way out, but I'm guessing that they aren't trying all that hard. They said they had plenty of food, lots of firewood, and enough liquor to last them until Valentine's Day."

"I appreciate you coming by, but you could have just called me," I told him.

"The truth of the matter is that I've always wanted to come by here, and this gave me the perfect excuse."

"You know what? Have three donuts," I said, laughing in relief that my husband was riding out the storm in good condition with old friends. It was more than I could have asked for.

"Thanks, but my limit's two," Kelly said with a grin. After he finished the second donut and refilled his coffee cup, he actually tipped an imaginary hat to me. "Now that I've been here, I'll be back."

"That's great, but next time, you should know that you'll probably have to pay," I said with a smile.

"Isn't that always the way?" he asked me with a grin. "They get you hooked, and then you're a goner. It's fine with me. These are worth every penny I'll be paying for them in the future. You have yourself a nice day, ma'am."

"You too, Kelly."

We finally ran out of donuts, and there were not enough supplies on hand to make any more. Besides, most of the town had power again, and the cleanup crews had done a marvelous job. We'd lost some trees, but besides Greg Whitmore, there hadn't been any ice-storm fatalities, and I didn't think it was fair to blame the weather for what had happened to the victim. My suppliers had all been champions, and Melissa's delivery woman was due at any moment. I sent everyone home, with my extreme thanks, and sat out front on one of the folding chairs waiting for the supplies to show up. The donut shop was looking a little down in the dumps after the frontal assault from the tree, but I promised myself that I'd make it better than it had been before. I tried playing with ideas for the remodeling, since I was going to have to do it anyway, but my flair was more about pastry treats than it was about what color went with what. I knew that Grace would be able to help me, and so would Momma, so I didn't worry about what would come later. The temporary fixes would hold me for a while, but I knew that I'd want permanent solutions soon.

I was still pondering things I might do when there was a tap at the door. My flour, along with other essential supplies, had arrived! After everything was put away, I buttoned the shop up and headed home to take a quick shower. It had been a long, hard morning, and I needed to clean up even more than I needed a nap. As I walked through the park, I couldn't help but glance over at the bench where Grace and I had found Greg. Had it honestly just happened that morning? The temperature had warmed up enough so that chunks of ice had dropped off the trees in the sunlight, and there was no record in the grass that it had ever been coated with ice.

That turned out not to be entirely true, though.

A burst of sunlight peeking out from the clouds seemed to illuminate two lines in the grass that led straight to Greg's bench.

What was that about? Could it have been my imagination? I stopped where I'd first seen it and walked back to the bench. Sure enough, if I held my head just right, I could make out two tracks spaced eighteen inches apart leading directly to Greg's bench. There was still ice in each narrow path, though it had melted everywhere else the sunshine had hit. I took out my phone, more as a matter of habit than anything else, and snapped a few pictures. The only problem was that I couldn't get the lines to show up in the shots. I finally took an extreme close-up that showed a small section of one line, and I managed to capture the image. Taking out a dollar bill, I placed it between the tracks and took a few more photos, hoping to show the spacing correctly.

It was time to call the police chief before the track vanished entirely.

"Chief Grant, this is Suzanne Hart. I need you."

"What's going on, Suzanne? Are you already in trouble?"

"I resent that remark, as much as I might resemble it at times," I replied. "There's something you need to see at the park, and you need to get over here as quickly as you can."

"I can be there in twenty minutes," he said with a sigh.

"You might as well not come at all then, if that's the best you can do," I answered.

"Are you sassing me, woman?" he asked, trying to hide his vexation with me.

"No, sir. I just meant that the sun is going to wipe out these tracks before you get here."

"The twin lines in the ice? I saw them," he replied.

"What do you make of them, Chief?" I asked him.

"I'm not ready to say just yet."

"Are you being cagey with me, sir?"

"No, ma'am. I wouldn't do that, ma'am." Was he poking at me by calling me ma'am repeatedly?

"Okay, I just thought you should know about them if you

hadn't noticed them already." My tone was curt, and he clearly picked up on it.

Before I could hang up, he said, "Suzanne, I appreciate you calling me. If I hadn't seen them myself, I would have loved hearing about them from you."

"No worries," I said, remembering the burden my young friend had on his shoulders as our chief of police. "They look like lines made by ice skates, but nobody would be skating out in the park in the middle of an ice storm." And then I knew what they had to have been. "Stephen, why would someone be out pulling an old-fashioned snow sled in the middle of an ice storm? It doesn't make sense."

"Suzanne, you haven't called me Stephen since the mayor made me the police chief," he said with amusement in his voice.

"Stop trying to change the subject. You knew it was from a sled, didn't you? Is that how the killer got the body out to the park?"

He hesitated a few moments before answering. "Probably. That's good detective work, Suzanne."

"Well, at least you didn't call me ma'am again," I said with a smile.

"Sorry about that. We're canvassing the neighborhoods right now looking for a sled. It might be nice if we could get a bead on where it came from, but the tracks were gone as soon as the sled hit the sidewalk. So far, we haven't had any luck locating it yet, but I have faith that it will turn up sooner or later. Keep it on your radar as you go around chatting with people this afternoon, okay?"

"You bet," I said. "Have you spoken with Lori again yet?"

"Twice, as a matter of fact," the chief answered. "You know, I wouldn't mind if you and Grace took a run at her, too. You might be able to get more out of her than I've been able to."

"We'd be happy to give it a shot," I said, quickly agreeing to the proposal.

"You know this is still all unofficial, right?" he asked.

"Of course I do. Chief, I could take classes all day long in forensics at the college and still not be a detective. Grace and I are good with people, not the science of crime solving. We'll leave that to you pros who train your entire lives for it."

"Don't discount the value you two add," the chief said magnanimously.

"Oh, we don't. I just don't want you thinking that we believe for one second that we could do what you do. If we can add a little to the mix, that's great, and I admit that we uncover answers sometimes ourselves, but no one wants us to take your place, especially not us."

"I appreciate that. Hey, take it easy with Lori, okay? She's a bit of a wreck right now, even if she and Greg *were* in the process of splitting up."

"We'll be as gentle as we can be," I told him. "Thanks for the vote of confidence."

"No worries. Happy hunting."

After we hung up, I marveled at how well Grace and I worked with the new chief of police. Jake had quit the temporary post when he'd had a conflict with my team and me in particular, but Stephen seemed to be willing to use us in a limited, and extremely unofficial, capacity.

I suddenly realized that we had another book club meeting coming up at the donut shop the next day. I wondered if the gracious ladies in my club would mind the folding chairs instead of the comfortable couch and padded seats we usually enjoyed, but then I realized that I was probably worrying for nothing. The ladies would be focused first on the mystery, and second, my treats. If anything, it would add a little more spice to our conversation about weathering the storm. The meeting was nearly upon me, and I still hadn't finished the book, but I wasn't all that worried about it. With Jake out of town, even with an investigation of my own to conduct, I'd finish it in time. I wasn't sure what it was about the mystery we'd chosen, but I was having the toughest time getting into it. Maybe the women in the group would have some insights as to why I was having so much trouble.

I got home to find Grace sitting in her car with the engine running.

When I approached her vehicle, I saw that she was doing paperwork. I tapped on the glass and, in the process, nearly scared her to death. After shutting off the engine, she got out and frowned at me. "Are you trying to give me a heart attack, Suzanne?"

"Sorry. I was going to come by and get you as soon as I grabbed a shower," I said, not mentioning the fact that I'd been considering taking a twenty-minute power nap as well. "Why didn't you wait for me inside?"

"It's locked," she said, "and I didn't want to miss you by staying at my place."

"Come on in, then," I said.

Once we were inside the cottage, I noticed that several of the lights we'd had on when the power had gone out the night before had come to life, including the movie we'd been watching. The screen had a randomly moving logo now, the movie long since playing itself out. I shut it off as I put my coat on the couch. "I'm going to grab a quick shower before we do anything else, okay?"

"Mind if I do a little more work on the kitchen table while I'm waiting?" she asked me.

"Be my guest. If you have to go in to work today, it's fine with me."

Grace grinned. "Now why on earth would I do that? If I put in another fifteen minutes, I don't have to take a vacation day."

"You really love your job, don't you?"

"You know it, almost as much as you love yours," she replied. "Have a good shower. Did you speak with Stephen? Did he tell you we had his blessing to talk to Lori Whitmore?"

"He did," I said. "No worries. I won't be long."

"Like I said, take your time," she answered.

CHAPTER 8

THE SHOWER WASN'T AS GOOD as a nap, but it still managed to help rejuvenate me. I took the time to dry my hair thoroughly before I joined Grace. There was no sense going out into the cold with it wet, even if I knew that the old wives' tale about chilly weather causing colds wasn't true. Momma had ingrained it into me as a child, and that made it fact, whether it was actually true or not.

After getting completely ready, I found Grace collecting her papers and shoving them into her briefcase. "Perfect timing. I just finished up."

"You know, you could always just *tell* them you put in the time," I told her with a grin.

"Sorry, that's not going to happen. I might play fast and loose with some of the company's policies, but that's one I happen to agree with." Grace took in my clean clothes and shiny hair. "My, don't you look nice."

I noticed that her casual attire was still classier than my finest dress. The woman could sleep in her clothes and still look better than I could if I had an hour with a professional stylist. "Right back at you," I said. "Are you ready to tackle Lori?"

"It's not going to be easy, but it needs to be done. Do you think she could have actually killed her husband?"

"I'm sure it happens more than we realize," I said as we walked outside. "Should I drive us over there?"

"In Jake's truck? You're kidding, right?"

"I didn't think you were supposed to take your company car out on personal business," I reminded her.

"That's where I consider the policy more of a suggestion than an actual rule," she answered with a grin. I wasn't about to argue situational ethics with Grace.

"Come on," I urged her. "Climb in. It's not so bad, and Jake has four heavy sandbags in back for extra weight, not to mention brand-new tires. We'll be fine."

"If you say so," Grace said skeptically. Once she climbed in, she smiled at me. "This isn't nearly as bad as I was expecting."

"I'm sure if Jake were here to hear that, he'd be gushing with pride right about now."

"Speaking of your husband, have you had any more word from him?"

"As a matter of fact, he managed to get a message out to me through a ham radio operator. Everyone at the party is fine. Evidently they're all hunkering down at the lodge and probably having the time of their lives. I doubt they've even noticed they are snowed in. When you get that many ex-law-enforcement folks together, the shoptalk alone would curl your toes."

"I'm just happy that he's okay," she said.

"We're all good on that front," I said as I drove us to where Lori was staying. She'd moved out of the home she'd shared with Greg in town and was now living with her best friend, Penny Parsons. Penny was a nurse at the hospital and a friend of mine as well. She hadn't been in her place long either, moving to be closer to work a year earlier.

I was surprised when Penny answered the door after we knocked. "I thought you'd be at the hospital," I said.

"I just got off my shift," she said, looking quite a bit worse for wear. "Why are you here, Suzanne, Grace? Strike that. I just realized why. It's Lori, isn't it? She can't talk to you, ladies."

"What makes you think we're here to see Lori?" Grace asked her.

"My mistake. Are you here to see Lori?"

I wasn't about to lie to my friend. "Yes."

Penny frowned before she answered. "Like I said, she's a mess. Evidently the police chief has been grilling her off and on for hours, and she's in no shape to talk to you two."

"Who is it, Penny?" a woman's voice called out from the living room.

"Girl Scouts out on a cookie run," the nurse said, openly scowling at us now and daring us to dispute what she'd just said.

"Girl Scouts don't sell cookies this time of year," the woman said as she joined us. I wouldn't say she looked particularly happy to see us standing there, but she didn't seem all that surprised by our presence, either. "I wondered when you two would get around to talking to me. You're looking into what happened to Greg, aren't you?"

"We are," I said. This was no time for subterfuge, though Grace and I used that as well occasionally during the course of our investigations.

"You might as well come in, then," she said.

Penny didn't move, though. "Lori, you know that you're under no obligation to speak with them. You've had a rough day. If you ask me, I'd say don't do it."

I couldn't blame Penny for protecting her friend, but I couldn't just let her turn us away without a fight, either. "Lori, you loved him once, and you can't deny it. Don't you want to help us find his killer?" I asked her.

"Suzanne, that's not fair, and you know it," Penny said, scolding me.

"How is that not fair?" Grace asked her.

"She's in no condition to have a conversation with you," Penny insisted.

Lori touched her friend's arm. "Do you honestly think there's one chance in a thousand that they won't come back here tomorrow, or the next day, or the one after that?" she asked the nurse softly.

"No," Penny said, and then she turned to us. "No offense."

"None taken," I said with a slim smile. "Believe me, it's important, or we wouldn't ask."

"Fine. It's up to you, Lori. As for me, I'm going to bed."

"We'll try to keep it down," Lori said as Penny started to disappear into a back room.

"I've been on my feet twenty-six straight hours. You could set off a cannon in here and I wouldn't hear it."

"Thanks, Penny," I called out.

"Don't thank me," she said sleepily. "If it were up to me, you'd still be standing outside wondering what just happened."

I laughed at her comment, which was the perfect response. "Good night."

"Night," we all echoed. I looked around the place after Penny left. The only sign that Christmas was close was a sad little artificial tree no more than three feet tall sitting on the coffee table.

Once the nurse was safely ensconced in her room, Lori said, "I'd offer you something to drink, but this isn't my place. Penny has been kind enough to let me stay here, but I'm careful not to overstep my welcome." The recent widow collapsed onto the couch, and then she said glumly, "So, you want to talk about Greg. Fine. What do you want to know?"

"Who would want to hurt him?" I asked her gently.

"Do you mean besides me?" she asked as she shrugged. "Don't bother denying it. I know that's what you two are thinking. So is the police chief, for that matter."

"We understand that just because you were splitting up doesn't necessarily mean that you wanted to see him dead," Grace told her.

"Tell that to your boyfriend, then."

"I'm sure he's just following procedure," Grace began to explain when Lori cut her off.

"It's okay. I don't blame him, but I don't have to like it either, do I?"

"No. I understand completely," Grace said.

"So, you want to know who else might want to kill Greg. The truth is that's all I've been thinking about since I first heard the news. Believe me, it doesn't make any sense."

"So, you don't know anyone who might be holding a grudge against him?" I asked her incredulously. I didn't know *anyone* who went through life without collecting at least a few folks who wouldn't shed a tear if tragedy befell them.

Lori pondered my question for a few seconds before she answered. "Did Greg have enemies? Sure. Who doesn't? But putting a bullet in him and dumping his body in the park wasn't exactly a proportional response to being snubbed or treated rudely, do you know what I mean?"

"His body wasn't just dumped," I reminded her. "Someone went to great pains to set him up on a park bench to make it seem as though he were one of the town's plastic Santas. Why go to that much trouble?"

"You'll have to ask the killer, but I assumed it was to make it take longer for someone to discover the body. The police chief showed me a picture of him, if you can believe that, and I didn't have any idea it was Greg, and I was married to the man. If you and Grace hadn't been walking close by, would anyone have realized what was happening until later?"

"Maybe not," I said. It was an interesting point, especially for the widow to be making. "You don't happen to own a sled, do you? Or Penny?"

Lori looked puzzled by the question. "The chief of police asked me the same thing."

"And what did you say?" Grace asked her.

"I told him no, but what could it possibly matter?"

I decided to skip answering that particular question. After all, there was no need for her to know just yet that her husband's dead body had been sledded out to the park in the middle of the ice storm. "It's just one of the things we need to know. Okay, so you say you don't know anyone who would want to kill him. I can respect that, but surely there must be *someone* who's not pleased with him."

After sitting there a few seconds, she said, "I know he and his boss have been having problems lately. Calvin Trinket has been threatening to fire Greg, and my husband seemed to dare him to go through with it. Something's going on there, but I don't have a clue what it might be."

"Where exactly did your husband work?" I asked her. I knew Greg commuted out of town, but I didn't know where he went every day or even what he did for a living. It had just never come up during any of our many interactions. He bought donuts, I sold donuts. It was usually as simple as that, with a little small talk thrown in for good measure.

"He was the assistant branch manager at Ninth Savings Bank in Union Square," she said proudly.

"Do you have any idea what the nature of the problems he was having with his boss might have been?" Grace asked her.

"I asked him a few times, but I never got a straight answer out of him. Greg and I weren't really all that close over the past few months."

"What happened between the two of you? Do you mind me asking?" I knew it wasn't any of my business, but I was having a hard time understanding how love could just die like that.

Lori looked as though she wanted to cry, but she managed to hold it in. "All I know for sure is that it takes two people to want a marriage to work. After his car wreck and his time in the hospital, things were never the same between us."

"Did he just give up on you, or was there someone new in his life?" Grace asked her gently.

"No! Never! Not Greg. He wouldn't have done that to me. I honestly don't know what happened. He refused to share whatever was happening to him with me."

"I'm curious about something," I said. "If Greg was the reason for your separation, why were you the one who moved out?"

Lori bit her lower lip for a moment before answering. "It was his mother's house to begin with. Even if he would have offered it to me, I wouldn't have stayed there. What I needed was a clean break."

Well, she'd gotten that, I thought to myself, though I never would have voiced it. "How about Greg's friends? Can you think of anyone else we should talk to?"

"The only one he was still close to was Benny Young. They worked together at the bank. Talk to him. He might know something."

We were interrupted as Penny came out of the bedroom, looking irritated with the world. "Okay, I was wrong."

"About letting us in?" I asked her.

"No, that's Lori's business, but your voices are carrying into the bedroom, and I'm having trouble getting to sleep. Give me a break, would you?"

I stood, and Grace followed suit. "Sorry. We'll leave."

She nodded. "Thanks. You know I'm not ordinarily this cranky, right?" Penny asked us with a grin.

"If I'd worked the shift you just pulled, I'd be spraying us with a water hose to get us to leave," I reassured her. Turning to Lori, I said, "If you think of anything or anyone else, let me know." I handed her one of my donut shop cards, and Grace and I were soon back in Jake's truck.

"That was interesting," I said.

"You bet it was. She didn't tell us everything she knows, did she?"

I looked at Grace oddly for a moment before I answered. "I'm not sure what you're talking about. Did I miss something? What did you pick up on that I didn't?"

"Don't you think she protested the absence of a girlfriend in her husband's life a little too vigorously?"

I thought about it, and then I shrugged. "I'm not sure."

"Well, I am. Something's not right there."

"At least we know she doesn't have an alibi for the time of the murder," I added as I started driving.

Grace nodded. "I almost didn't put that together at first. Penny told us up front that she'd been working at the hospital the entire time of the ice storm. It would have been easy for Lori to sneak over to her former home, shoot her husband, and then take his body to the park and get back to Penny's before anyone even knew she was gone."

"When you say it like that, it sounds pretty complicated, doesn't it? Why didn't she just shoot him and leave him where he was?"

Grace answered, "When a spouse is murdered, who is the first person they speak with? Who has Stephen interviewed repeatedly?"

"Lori," I said.

"If Greg had been found at home, wouldn't it have looked even more like Lori could be involved? By leaving his body in the park, it opens up the list of people who might have done it."

"I can see that, but why risk carting him on a sled in the middle of an ice storm? What if someone saw her?"

"I'm guessing if anyone had been out to see it, it probably would have looked as though they were out trying to enjoy the icy weather."

"You can't sled in an ice storm," I reminded her.

"Au contraire. At college, we'd slide on cafeteria trays in a heavy rain. Ice would have been welcome if snow weren't available."

"Either way, we need to keep her high on our list."

Grace looked around. "Where are we going, anyway?"

"I'd say a trip to the bank is in order, wouldn't you?"

"Sure, but we can't just barge in asking questions about Greg without some kind of explanation."

"We can't?" I asked her with a slight smile. "I thought you enjoyed role-playing."

"That's an entirely different matter. We haven't done that in a while. Who are we going to be this time? I know. How about sisters who have just inherited millions and need advice on how to best invest it?"

"I was thinking of something a little less spectacular than that," I admitted.

"What did we do, inherit thousands? That won't get us nearly as much attention."

"Let's settle on an even fifty thousand dollars," I said. "I'm guessing that Greg handled more than just loans. He might do some low-dollar investments as well. We were going to consult with him, but we'll insist on speaking with the branch manager himself."

"Okay, I'd buy that. Now, what should our names be? I always fancied myself as Francisca Dubois."

I had to laugh at such an outlandish name. "Really? Do I call you Frannie for short?"

"Not if you expect me to answer. You can be Myrtle."

"Do I look like a Myrtle to you? And be careful how you answer that. Our friendship might be riding on it."

"No," she conceded, "but you made fun of my name."

"Why don't I be Helen?" I suggested.

"Fine by me, Helen. This is going to be fun."

"Remember, we're still investigating a murder, Grace."

"I know, but that doesn't mean we can't enjoy ourselves a little in the process. And you mean Francisca, don't you?"

"Sorry, Francisca, my mistake."

"That's better," she said with a grin.

CHAPTER 9

"**L**ADIES, I'M SORRY TO INFORM you that Mr. Whitmore won't be able to help you this afternoon," Calvin Trinket said as he approached us.

"Why ever not? Was he delayed by the ice storm?" I asked innocently.

"Fortunately, we were lucky to be spared its wrath here," the bank manager said. "Was there something that I might be able to help you with?"

We'd informed the woman up front that we had an appointment with Greg, and she looked puzzled for a moment before excusing herself and going straight to the branch manager's office. The moment she was gone, I looked around the lobby and was amazed to find just how nondenominationally they'd managed to celebrate the season. There was no sign of a Christmas tree of any kind, but there were several large paper snowflakes on display, as well as enough stringed garland to cover city hall and still have enough left over to wrap the town clock. Calvin Trinket had come out almost immediately after the receptionist had told him we were there. He was a short, heavyset man with graying hair who waddled more than he walked.

"Oh, dear," Grace said, being a little too overdramatic for my taste. "We did so trust Mr. Whitmore. Has he left your employ?"

"Unfortunately, he met with an untimely accident," Calvin said smoothly. I'd never heard anyone being shot categorized as an accident, but let him spin things the way he wanted to. "Still,

I'd be more than happy to assist you. I understand it's a rather modest sum."

"Just fifty thousand," Grace said with open ease. "It's such a small fraction of our overall estate it was hardly worth bothering our regular advisors with. My sister and I have grown a little uneasy with our current financial consultants, so if this is handled well, we might be open to shifting some of our larger assets to your bank as well."

The man was virtually licking his lips at the news. Maybe Grace had been right. Going in with the premise of investing a modest sum had made sense to me at the time, but this was one case where Grace's flair might pay off. "Please, follow me into my office."

After we were settled in and before Calvin could start his sales pitch for his financial services, I said, "If you don't mind, we'd like to talk a little bit about Mr. Whitmore. After all, it was his presence that made us interested in your establishment in the first place."

Calvin was not used to being thwarted, that much was obvious by his reaction. "What is there to say? I'm not at liberty to discuss his situation, but suffice it to say that it has nothing to do with this institution."

This was getting us nowhere. It may have been a mistake approaching him in this manner, but it was too late to change strategies now. Or was it? I let my face go slack as I asked, "Is there perhaps a restroom I could use? I'm not feeling entirely well."

"Of course," he said.

As he gave me directions, I winked at Grace, who nodded gravely and put a hand on my arm. "Should I go with you?"

"No, you stay here. I shan't be long." What had gotten into me? I'd never said "shan't" before in my life.

I started for the restroom, stayed a moment or two when I got there, and then I headed back, lingering at Calvin's assistant's desk along the way. The plaque said her name was Gwen West. Young and pretty, she was voluptuous without being very overweight, and I knew from experience that type of girl would be watching her calories for the rest of her life, or she would someday find herself dismayed to find that none of her clothes fit her anymore and that the men weren't nearly as attentive as they'd once been. She'd clearly been crying, and I imagined she was the one I really should talk to about Greg Whitmore and not the man's former boss.

"Are you all right, my dear?" I asked her gently.

"I'm fine. It's just allergies," she said as she dabbed at her eyes.

"In December? It doesn't have anything to do with Mr. Whitmore's unfortunate accident, does it?"

"Why do you ask?" she asked me suspiciously.

"Your Mr. Trinket doesn't seem to be a very big fan of the man, but I'm guessing that you were," I confided in her.

"He wouldn't," she said acidly as she glanced back critically in her boss's direction. "He was doing his best to get rid of Greg, and now, all of a sudden, someone shoots him in the back of the head. It just doesn't make sense, if you ask me."

My, my, word traveled fast. I hadn't even realized any civilians besides Grace and I even knew what had really happened to Greg. "How did you learn that?"

"Benny told me," she said as she pointed toward a man sitting a hundred feet away from us. In a hushed voice, she added, "If you ask me, the police should be talking to Calvin."

"Would he have done something so drastic just to get rid of an employee?" I asked her, doing my best to empathize with the poor woman.

"All I know for sure is that there was something going on with a few of Greg's loans. My guess is that he wanted to increase the amounts on them, but Calvin wouldn't approve any of his requests. I heard them yelling two nights ago after everyone else had gone home. I wouldn't have been here at all myself, but I forgot my purse, and I had to come back for it." She stopped speaking abruptly, and I felt someone's presence directly behind me. For a heavy man, Calvin Trinket certainly had a light footstep. "Thank you, my dear," I said loudly to Gwen, and entirely for his benefit. "I appreciate the advice. My sister and I definitely will try Napoli's while we're in town." I turned and acted surprised to find Calvin standing in front of me. "Your assistant was kind enough to recommend a restaurant to us while we're here," I said. "Gwen's a real jewel."

"We think so," he said, trying to decide if I was telling the truth or lying. Good luck with that, bub.

"They really are delightful," Gwen said a little too enthusiastically.

"Mr. Trinket," I started when we got back to his office.

He interrupted me. "Please, call me Calvin."

"Calvin, then. I just remembered something. Mr. Whitmore instructed us that if he couldn't meet with us for any reason, we should speak with a Mr. Young. I trust he is available."

"He is, but I assure you, I'm the one you need to deal with." He said it with a finality that offered no recourse but to accept his word as gold, but clearly he'd never dealt with my best friend before.

"So, are you saying that you won't allow it?" Grace asked him, putting just the right amount of frost in her voice.

"I wouldn't say that," Calvin backpedaled quickly. "I honestly believe that if you deal with anyone at our fine institution, it needs to be me."

Grace took that in, and then she stood and joined me. "Very well, then. If that's your decision, I won't stay here and argue with you. Have a pleasant day, Mr. Trinket. Come, Helen, there are other banks to visit."

We didn't even make it out of his office door before he spoke up. "I'm sorry, I must not have explained myself clearly. Of course you can speak with whomever you'd like. In fact, I'll show you to Mr. Young's office myself," he said swiftly.

"I don't know if that's necessary at this point," Grace said, clearly displaying her unhappiness with his earlier behavior. What was she doing?

"Gra...great day, sister dear. Let's give him a chance." I'd nearly called her by her real name, and I'd only barely managed to cover it by creating an expression that no one in their right mind would ever use.

"Very well. If you insist," she said. "Lead on, Mr. Trinket."

Calvin looked relieved by our acceptance of his offer. "You won't be sorry. Follow me, please."

As we left the manager's office, I slowed to smile at Gwen, who looked as though she'd regretted sharing anything with me. I wanted to stop and assure her that I wouldn't use any of it, but that would be a bald-faced lie. What she'd confided in me might be very valuable indeed.

Benny Young was the antithesis of his boss, young and slick and handsome in an oily kind of way. He took his boss's introduction of us in stride, offered his hand to each of us, and then showed us to his seats. He started to say something to Grace, but she shook her head quickly, and whatever he was about to say died in his throat. Calvin stayed put in the doorway, something we couldn't have if we were going to grill Benny. "You may leave us, Mr. Trinket," I said, trying to match Grace's frosty voice.

He looked embarrassed, as though he'd been caught sneaking a peek into the girls' locker room. "Of course. Call if you need me."

We both nodded, and soon enough, we had the man all to ourselves. "Benny, first of all, you should know that we are here under false pretenses," Grace said, her blunt honesty nearly knocking me off my chair. What happened to our role-playing, and why had she abandoned it so suddenly? I wanted to protest, but Grace's instincts were usually pretty accurate when it came to sizing up people.

"Okay, I'll bite," he said with a conspiratorial smile. "Why are you really here?"

"We're investigating Greg Whitmore's murder," I said, matching Grace's bluntness with my own. "We were told you were his best friend."

"Yeah, that's true enough," Benny said, his smile dying on his lips. "I can't believe someone shot him down like he had rabies or something."

"Where did you hear what happened to him?" I asked.

"I play basketball with a guy from the coroner's office," he explained. "As soon as he found out where Greg worked, he called me. It's the darnedest thing. I still can't believe it really happened."

"Do you have any idea who would do such a thing?" Grace asked him.

"You should talk to Lori, his wife," Benny said glumly.

"We already have," I volunteered. "Do you think she might have done it?"

"They didn't get along, that's for sure. When she found out Greg was dating someone before they were even divorced, she nearly lost it in the parking lot a few days ago."

Lori knew there was someone else in her husband's life? She'd lied to us? Why? "Do you know who he was seeing?"

"Well, it wasn't exactly a secret around here," Benny said as he pointed to Gwen West, who was watching us closely.

"He was dating Trinket's assistant?" I asked.

"Well, I suppose it was his turn," Benny said with a frown.

"What do you mean by that?"

"Let's just say that Gwen has gone out with a few of us over the past few years," he said.

"Including you?" Grace asked him.

Her shot scored a direct hit, based on his reaction. "Sure, we went out a few times, but everybody knew that Greg was the one she had her eye on. When he finally agreed to go out with her, that was the end of us."

"So, you're telling us that your best friend stole your girlfriend," I said. What was this, high school?

"No, it was nothing like that. Gwen and I went out two or three times, but there weren't any real sparks there. Now she and Greg, they had a passionate relationship. They were either screaming at each other or making out in the supply closet, and you never knew which it would be from day to day. Shoot, hour to hour, truth be told."

"So, there was no friction between the two of you?" I asked him.

"We were pals," Benny said with a shrug. "So, there's really no money to invest?"

"I'm afraid not," I said.

"Man, Calvin is going to be all over me. Our deposits are down, and he's going to accuse me of blowing it," Benny said sadly. "Great. Here he comes."

I pivoted to see the manager approach us, and I came up with something on the spot that might help. When I was certain Trinket could hear us, I said, "When we decide to invest, you'll be the first one we contact. I'm sorry we can't stay longer, but I'm really not feeling well at all." I was turning on my fake illness so much that I was actually starting to feel queasy.

"May we call you a doctor?" Calvin asked solicitously as he joined us. Man, he wasn't going to let us go easily.

"Thank you, but no. No one cares for us but our family physician."

Grace hustled me out of the building, and I was half afraid the branch manager might follow us out. What would he think about our supposed fortune if he saw us driving away in Jake's old beat-up pickup truck? Fortunately, Gwen called out to him that he had a phone call, and he left us before he made it out the door.

"Quick, let's go," I said, urging Grace to move before the branch manager could find out what we were really driving away in.

"What's the rush?" she asked, even though she did as I'd requested. "You're acting as though we're robbing the place."

As I started the engine, praying that it didn't choose this moment to die, I asked, "Let me ask you something. Would Francisca be caught dead in this truck?"

"She most certainly would not," Grace said haughtily, and then she grinned. "I can't believe you almost called me by my real name in Trinket's office."

"Great day, it's hard not to," I said, using my own idiom again. Who knew? Maybe it would catch on, but I doubted it.

"What did you get from the assistant?" Grace asked me. "That was pretty slick getting suddenly sick and excusing yourself, by the way."

"Thank you, ma'am," I said. "Gwen claimed that Greg and Calvin were fighting about some loans. Evidently Greg wanted something changed, but Calvin refused. I wonder if there was something fishy about them."

"I don't know. Were you surprised when Benny told us that Greg was dating Gwen?"

"Why, because she was a good twenty-five years younger than he was?" I asked. "Nothing surprises me about dating these days. I didn't quite buy Benny's calm acceptance about being dumped though, did you?"

"He couldn't have taken it as casually as he pretended to, that's for sure," she said.

"I still can't believe Lori lied to us about that," I answered as

I found myself heading to Napoli's. Talking about it had made me want it.

"Could she have lied to us out of pride? It had to be humiliating for her to be dumped for someone so much younger," Grace said. "In fact, the more I think about it, the more I find that I don't blame her for lying to us." She looked around and asked, "Hey, are we going to eat at Napoli's?"

"I thought I might get something to take home, if you don't mind," I said.

"Forget that," Grace said with a grin. "It's a lot better when it's hot and fresh, and you know it. I've been dreaming about Angelica's lasagna for weeks."

"I just figured you might have plans with Stephen tonight, especially since we had our slumber party last night."

"Suzanne, you know how he is when he's working on a case. I won't see him much until this is all over, so why shouldn't we enjoy a nice Italian meal out together?"

"If you're sure, there's no reason that I can think of," I answered with a grin.

CHAPTER 10

"LADIES, WHAT A SURPRISE," ANGELICA DeAngelis, the owner of Napoli's, greeted us as we walked in. She was a real beauty, ten years older than we were but still outshining nearly every woman in her presence. Angelica had four daughters, all of them beautiful in their own right, but none of them quite as lovely as their mother. The restaurant was decorated for the season, and there was no doubt in anyone's mind that the DeAngelis clan were believers in going over the top when it came to outfitting the place for the holidays.

"You're not cooking this evening?" I asked Angelica. It was rare to find the woman out of her kitchen at all.

"Tonight, my girls insist that they can handle things without me," she said loudly enough for her youngest, Sophia, to hear. In a softer voice, she told us with a smile, "In fact, they are doing beautifully. I'm so proud of my girls. Come, you may have my best table."

"I thought every table here was great," I told her with a grin as we followed her.

"Yes, of course," Angelica said, and then, in a quiet voice, she added, "Some are better than others, though." She snapped her fingers toward Sophia and pointed to us.

The youngest of the clan came over and smiled. "Hey, girls. What's up?"

"Sophia, is that any way to greet our customers?"

The young waitress stuck her tongue out at her mother,

and then she grinned. "Suzanne and Grace are a lot more than that, and you know it. Don't look now, but there are customers waiting to be seated."

Angelica noticed that she'd been remiss in her duties and scurried off without another word.

"I love when that happens," she said with a grin. "Now, what can I get you ladies?"

I didn't even need to look at the menu. "I'll have the lasagna. Ever since Grace mentioned it, I haven't been able to stop thinking about it."

"Make it two," Grace said with a smile.

"Would you both like your regular salads as well?"

"You'd better believe it," I said, "and bread, too. Lots of bread."

Sophia laughed. "No worries on that count. I know better than to come back to this table without fresh bread."

Once she was gone, Grace asked me, "What do you say, Suzanne? Should we make this a murder-free meal? A break from it might be nice."

"We can do whatever you'd like," I said.

"Why don't we, then?" Grace asked, and then she frowned for a moment. "That being said, there's something that's really bothering me. I realize that Lori was humiliated that Greg was dating a woman so much younger than she was, but what I don't get is why she was trying to protect her even after her husband was dead. Why on earth *wouldn't* she mention it to us? I'm starting to realize that mortification isn't enough of a reason to keep quiet about it."

"I can think of one reason," I said quietly.

"Why is that?"

"Knowing about Gwen gives Lori another motive for murder," I said.

"Wow, as if she needed any more than she already had."

"Are you talking about Greg Whitmore?" Sophia asked me as she brought us a basket spilling over with fresh bread. "It's terrible, isn't it?"

"Particularly since we're the ones who found the body," Grace said.

"I hadn't heard that part. Someone just said that he'd been shot in the park. He was wearing a snowman costume, is that right?"

"No, it was a Santa suit," I corrected her. How did these rumors and distortions get started?

"That makes more sense. But he was propped up on a bench in the park, right? Was that much at least right?"

"Yes, that's the way we found him," I said, shuddering a little at the memory. "Did you know him well?"

"Not that well, but he came here some, especially after he started dating Gwen West. I never would have believed that match if I hadn't seen it with my own two eyes."

"Why? Were they really that different? Besides the age thing, I mean."

Sophia shrugged. "I'm certainly no expert in love, but I didn't get it. I know that Gwen's dad abandoned the family when she was nine, and though she's gone out with men her own age in the past, it was clear that older men were her favorites."

That explained why she'd dumped Benny for Greg, or at least it provided one of the reasons. "How well did they get along in general?" I asked, wanting confirmation of Benny's interpretation of their story.

"Like oil and water," Sophia said. I could tell she wanted to add something to it, but then Angelica spotted her gossiping with us, and before her mother could join us, Sophia scooted away.

"Ladies, is everything okay here?" Angelica asked us.

"We're fine. We were just talking about Greg Whitmore."

The elegant older woman frowned, bit her lower lip, and then said, "It was a sad way to die."

"I understand he ate here occasionally," Grace said as nonchalantly as she could manage.

"Sophia's been talking again, I see," Angelica said sternly.

"Only because we asked her," I said, shading the truth a bit. I hated lying to my friend, but I didn't want to get her daughter in trouble, either.

"Actually, Sophia is the right one to speak with. She heard something the other night that was rather disturbing."

This might be good. "What did she overhear?"

"I think it's probably better for her to tell you herself." Angelica looked at the clock on the wall and suggested, "By the time you're finished with your meal, she'll be ready for her break. I'll have her speak with you then."

"We don't want to interfere with her time off," I said.

"This you'll want to hear," Angelica answered gravely, but we couldn't get anything more from her.

When Sophia brought us our food, she said hurriedly, "Mom told me to tell you what I heard. Meet me outside when you're finished. I know it's getting colder out there again, but I won't be long."

"Are you sure you wouldn't rather tell us now, in here where it's nice and warm?" Grace asked. She had never been a big fan of the cold.

"Things are really starting to hop in here, so the only way I'll be able to tell it is to step outside," Sophia said, and then she shivered a little. I knew it wasn't from the cold, since the restaurant was well heated, and I had to wonder if it concerned what she'd witnessed.

I was sure the food was just as good as always, but it was hard for me to focus on it, wondering what Angelica's youngest daughter had to tell us.

By the time we finished, Sophia brought us our checks, along with her coat. "Settle up, and I'll meet you outside."

I saw Antonia, one of Angelica's other daughters, leave the kitchen with an order pad, and she managed a smile in our direction before she got to work waiting tables. The girls prided themselves on being interchangeable, but I knew they each had their own specialties, and Antonia loved to cook.

As we paid for our meals, Angelica asked, "How was everything?"

I had my answer ready for her. "Good, but not as good as yours." I actually meant it, too, though the quality of the food wasn't necessarily a reflection on her daughters' expertise in the kitchen.

"That's the perfect answer, Suzanne," she said as she made change. "Where is that Jake of yours? Not that I'm not happy to see you here with her, Grace."

"He's snowed in at a bachelor party in the mountains," I said with a grin.

"Are there girls there?" Angelica asked disapprovingly.

"No, he's with half a dozen ex-state police investigators. I'm guessing they're discussing their glory days and the goriest cases they ever had."

"That doesn't sound much like a party to me," Angelica said with distaste.

"Exactly. That's why I came here with Grace."

"Well, come back anytime. Now, go, you two. Sophia is waiting for you."

"Thanks, Angelica," I said as I hugged her.

She beamed as she returned it. "It's always a pleasure seeing you both, and you know it. You ladies don't be strangers now, you hear?"

"No, ma'am. We wouldn't dream of it," Grace said happily. Angelica really did make us both feel as though we were two of her own girls, which was the greatest compliment she could pay us, and we were both well aware of it.

Sophia was outside stamping her feet together and rubbing her hands.

"Sorry we kept you waiting out in the cold," I said.

"When my mother gets to chatting with the two of you, I would expect nothing else. Okay, I don't have a ton of time, so here goes."

And then she proceeded to tell us exactly what she'd witnessed two nights earlier.

"Greg and Gwen have been coming here off and on for years but never together. At least until recently, that is. Three weeks ago, they started coming here together most evenings for dinner. Some nights they acted as though they were so in love I could barely stand to be around them, you know what I mean?"

"I do," Grace said, and I nodded. There were some people who brandished their feelings like sabers, daring anyone to complain about their displays of affection. I took comfort in seeing a hug here or a kiss there, but there was clearly such a thing as too much of what Emma liked to call excessive PDA, public displays of affection.

"But then there were other nights where I was afraid to give them sharp knives. I've never understood those kinds of relationships that are so volatile. Some people think it's being passionate. I think it's being a little crazy."

"Do you think either one of them was actually unbalanced?" I asked her. I'd just met Gwen, but she'd seemed reasonable enough, and in all the time I'd known Greg, I'd never thought of him as being irrational. Maybe they were fine apart, but when they got together, they brought out the best, or more likely the worst, in each other.

"Mr. Whitmore was always fine, but Gwen has been overly

dramatic for as long as I've known her. Anyway, this all leads up to what I saw a few nights ago. We had closed for the night, and I was working the front, cashing out the register, when I heard yelling in the parking lot. We don't get many drunks here, but my mother is strict about our image, so I knew she wouldn't want anything going on in our parking lot. As soon as I opened the front door, I could hear Gwen and Greg screaming at each other at the top of their lungs. They were having a fight to end all fights."

"What was it about? Could you tell?" I asked her.

"I'm surprised you didn't hear it all the way in April Springs," Sophia said. "Gwen was shouting at Greg that he *had* to marry her, he had no choice, and he was answering loudly in no uncertain terms that he'd rather marry a wood-chipper than be tied to her for the rest of his life."

"She was pushing him that hard to get married? I didn't think they'd been dating that long," Grace asked.

"They hadn't, but evidently time was of the essence. I was about to say something when Gwen shouted something that stunned me into silence. 'The baby is yours, so whether you marry me or not, you're going to be chained to me for the rest of your life, whether you like it or not.' Wow, it caught Greg by surprise nearly as much as it did me!"

"She's *pregnant*?" I asked.

"So she said. Anyway, Greg yelled back at her, "I'd rather die than be chained to you," and she answered, "Be careful what you wish for," and then she stormed off on foot."

"What did Greg do?"

"He tried to talk to her, but she wouldn't have it. It was clear that he had calmed down some by then, but Gwen was ramped up like crazy. Anyway, the last I saw of them, he was following her down the street trying to discuss the situation with her, but she was still crazy upset. I didn't think much of it other than as something to tell my mother and my sisters, but then Greg was murdered, and I'm beginning to realize this is news someone else should hear."

"Have you called the police and told them about it?" Grace asked her.

"No. I didn't know who to contact."

Grace pulled out a pen and a sheet of paper from her purse and jotted a number down before handing it to Sophia. "This is Chief Grant's number. He's been here a dozen times before with me, Sophia. You can trust him."

"Okay. I'll call him," she said as she tucked the note into her apron.

"Right now," Grace insisted.

Sophia frowned. "Can't it wait half an hour? I have my dinner break then. If I call him now, I'll leave everyone inside shorthanded, and besides, it's not like Gwen's going anywhere between now and then."

Grace was about to answer when I butted in. "Half an hour will be fine," I said.

Sophia nodded her thanks, but Grace appeared to be a little put off by my advice. Once the youngest DeAngelis girl was back inside, my best friend asked me, "Why did you let her off the hook, Suzanne?"

"She's right, Grace. What's a half hour matter in the scheme of things? Besides, wouldn't you like to speak with Gwen first and find out what happened that night?"

"Of course I would, but how is Stephen going to feel about it if we do?"

"I imagine he'll be a little miffed at first, but I'm sure that he'll get over it." I glanced at my watch and saw that it was nearing six p.m. "If we hurry, we might be able to get to the bank before she leaves for the day. They have late hours today, don't they?"

"I think so," she said. "I'm still not quite sure we should do this."

"Stay in the car, then. It will give you complete deniability if Stephen asks you about it later."

"No thank you. If you're talking to her, then so am I."

"Then let's get going before we miss her completely and the point becomes moot."

CHAPTER 11

"Gwen, can we talk?" I asked the branch manager's assistant as Grace and I hurried to her on foot once we'd parked Jake's truck out of the way. The other employees were streaming out of the bank, and I saw Calvin Trinket start toward us as we approached her. In a low voice, I asked, "Do you really want your boss to hear us discuss the fight you had with Greg at Napoli's the other night?"

It worked like a charm as Gwen's face went white for a moment, and I worried that she might bolt on us right then and there, but she quickly regained her composure just as Calvin joined us. "Back again, ladies? I trust you are feeling better, Suzanne?"

"I'm doing okay," I said, and then I realized that he hadn't called me Helen. Someone must have told him the truth after we'd left. "Forgive our ruse earlier, but you never know who you can trust these days. I was afraid that if you knew who we were, you might not be as inclined to help, given the fact that my mother pulled her business from your bank last year." It was true, too. Momma had used the bank in Union Square as leverage against one in Maple Hollow to get more favorable conditions on her loans and had then promptly walked away, something I'd found out about by accident.

"I would never do that," Trinket said, doing his best to give me a smile. It was clear that he'd been expecting me to feel badly about lying to him, so my direct reply had thrown him off his game. "I can assure you that no matter what name you wish to invest under, your account will be kept entirely separate from any experiences we may have had with your mother in the past."

I smiled my best fake smile and stuck out my hand. "That's good to know, and I'll keep it in mind. Now, if you don't mind, Gwen was about to tell us about a place in Hickory that serves the best pie in seven counties."

He nodded. "Tim's Pie Palace? Yes, it's wonderful."

"Thanks again for coming over. I'm glad that everything is all out in the open now," I said, clearly dismissing him.

Trinket didn't know what else to do but leave us. "Very good then. Have a lovely evening."

"You, too," I said.

Grace smiled at me for an instant, and then we turned back to Gwen. "We've already heard all about the fight, so there's no use denying it."

"I won't apologize to anyone for my emotions. Greg and I had a passionate relationship," she told us. "Our arguments might have seemed heated to an outsider, but we both spoke from positions of love."

If that was love, I didn't want to have any part of it. I studied her flat belly for a moment, clearly defined by her tight dress, and then I said softly, "Forgive my impertinence, but how far along are you?"

"What? Oh. No, I'm not pregnant." Gwen said it with no shame or remorse, as though she'd said she wasn't a fan of modern poetry or jazz.

"But you told Greg you were," Grace pushed her.

"You have to understand the context," Gwen explained.

"We'd love to get the chance. Why don't you enlighten us?" I asked.

She frowned a moment before speaking, and when she did, there was still clear animosity in her voice. "He told me at dinner that he was enjoying our little fling. Well, I thought it was much more than that. When I asked him where he saw us in a year, he said glibly, 'Dating other people.' What can I say? I blew up. I thought we meant more to each other than that, so I decided to see if he really felt that way. I figured claiming to be pregnant would be a perfect barometer to see where things really stood between us."

"You didn't get the answer you were hoping for, did you?" I asked her softly. As insane as her ploy had been, it must have shattered her to realize that he wasn't all that interested in having any kind of long-term relationship with her.

"Don't kid yourself. He loved me. Greg spoke out of haste, and he regretted it the second he said it. I know what Sophia overheard, but she didn't follow us through town. Greg apologized, admitted that he'd overreacted, and that he'd been wrong to say what he'd said in the heat of the moment. I confessed that I really wasn't pregnant, and he understood why I'd said it, and he forgave me on the spot. No matter what you might think, the two of us had a future together, and someone robbed us of it."

"Did anyone else overhear that part of your conversation?" Grace asked her.

"No, I can't prove any of it, if that's what you're asking," she said huffily. "You'll just have to take my word for it."

"Gwen, where were you last night?" I asked gently.

"Are you asking me for an alibi?" she replied, her voice rising dramatically. I had clearly triggered something inside her.

"It might help if you had one," Grace added.

"It's none of your business! I wouldn't tell you if I was in bed with the mayor," she snapped as she stormed off in the direction of her car.

"The mayor would never put himself in that position," I said, defending George, even if she had been using hyperbole.

"You know what? I thought you were on my side, but you can both go bark at the moon as far as I'm concerned," she shouted before getting into her car and screeching out of the parking lot. We could at least testify to the existence of the woman's mercurial temper.

"That went well, didn't it?" Grace asked as soon as Gwen was gone. "Suzanne, we really should open a charm school together. We could offer classes on how to get along with anybody."

"Her outrage seemed a little too overly dramatic even for her, don't you think?" I asked, staring after her.

"What do you mean?"

"Think about it. Gwen was fine until we asked her for her alibi. Then, all of a sudden, she explodes and storms off. I don't know. It all seems a little too convenient to me, if you know what I mean."

"There are wheels within wheels within wheels," Grace said. "It's enough to make your head spin." As we walked back to Jake's truck, she asked, "Where does that leave us now?"

"Well, if it's all the same to you, I think we should head back to April Springs. We've given all of our suspects something to think about tonight, so why don't we let them brood about it, and we can tackle them again tomorrow? The more time they have to dwell on our conversations, the better, as far as I'm concerned."

"I know you're probably right, but I hate doing nothing. Isn't there anything we can do now?" she asked me.

"Let's use the drive home to talk about what we know, what we think, and what we believe might be possible."

"Is the trip going to be long enough for that?" she asked me with a smile.

"I don't know. Let's try it and see," I said as we got into the truck and headed back home.

"Grace, there's something I've been dying to ask you. Why did you come clean with Benny Young about why we were really there the moment we saw him?"

"That's easy enough to explain," Grace said. "I knew from the instant I saw him that he recognized me from an earlier encounter we had. No doubt that's how Trinket knew you were Suzanne and not Helen out in the parking lot."

"You two didn't go out once, did you?" I asked her. It was difficult seeing my stylish and sweet friend with a man who seemed so oily.

"What can I say? It was a blind date. I was promised a prince, but I got a frog instead. The man truly believes he is God's gift to women. How much must it have galled him to have Greg Whitmore steal his girl away from him? It had to be a crushing blow to his ego."

"He said that it wasn't that big a deal," I reminded her.

"What did you expect him to say? You don't know him like I do. It's motive for murder, as far as I'm concerned."

"But they were best friends," I protested, having a hard time grasping the concept that Benny could kill Greg Whitmore in cold blood.

"Which probably made it even worse. No, strike that. The absolute lowest point was probably having to see them canoodling in the closet at work together right under his nose."

"Canoodling?" I asked her, laughing. "Do people still canoodle?"

"Don't you?" she replied, chuckling along with me. "I know it's an old-fashioned word, but I think we should bring it back. It's at least as good as saying 'great day.'"

"Okay," I said, not sure that either phrase would ever catch on in this modern age. "So, jealousy gives Benny a motive. What about Trinket?"

"Gwen said that he and Greg were fighting about loans and that it got nasty. Could that be motive enough for murder?"

"It's possible," I said. "I can think of a couple of circumstances where it might prove to be fatal."

"I'd love to hear what they are," Grace said.

"To start with, what if Greg made dangerous loans that couldn't be paid back? He could have been pressured by bad people to do it, and he got caught."

"Okay, that's one possibility. What if Trinket discovered what he was up to? Or maybe we've got this whole thing backwards. What if Trinket was up to something? If the branch manager were covering his own tracks, killing Greg might make sense. After all, it would be hard for a dead man to deny he'd done anything wrong."

"I like the way your mind works," I said. "I'm sure there are other scenarios, but we have to keep Calvin Trinket on our list, at least until we find a compelling reason to drop his name from our group of suspects."

"Agreed. Do I even have to ask how you feel about Gwen's capacity for murder?"

"No," I said, shaking my head in disbelief. "I still find it hard to fathom the circumstances where she felt as though claiming to be pregnant when she wasn't was the act of a rational woman."

"She does seem to be at least a little crazy," Grace admitted. "I'm not sure I believe the murder method works for her, though."

"What, do you not think she could shoot someone? It's not because she's a woman, right?"

Grace shook her head. "We both know better than that. No, but if Gwen had done it, I'd take her more as a heat-of-the-moment kind of gal than a cold-blooded killer. If Greg had been shot in the heart, or even the face, half a dozen times, then I'd think Gwen might be more appropriate as a suspect."

I thought about that as I drove us back home, and then I came up with another scenario. "She had to know that if something happened to her boyfriend, the entire world would learn about their volatile relationship pretty fast, right?"

"Absolutely," Grace agreed. "So what?"

"What if she took that into account before she killed him? Shooting someone with one bullet in the back of the head seems cold and calculated. What if the murder wasn't a reckless act, though? What if she wanted him dead for rejecting her, but she was too smart to let her emotions get control of her?"

"I don't know. That's a lot of 'what ifs,' isn't it? We can't forget about Lori, either. She clearly wasn't at all happy about her ex-husband dating a much younger woman, she lied about knowing the affair had even happened, and to top it off, she lacks an alibi."

"Wow, when you put it that way, she should probably be sitting in jail right now," I said.

"I'm not saying that she actually did it," Grace corrected me quickly. "All I'm saying is that she at least deserves a place on our list."

"Who could have dreamed that Greg's life was so complicated?" I asked as we neared the city limit sign of April Springs.

"It just goes to show you. We often don't know much about the people on the edges of our lives, do we?"

"On that profound note, I think we should put a pin in this until tomorrow after work. What's your schedule look like tomorrow?"

"I have more paperwork to do, but I can work around our investigation."

Jake was still gone, and I didn't relish spending the night alone. "Do you have any plans tonight?"

"I'm free as a bird," she said, and then her cell phone announced that she had a text. "Hang on one second." After a moment, she said, "Can you believe it? Stephen wants to come over. You can come in, too, if you'd like."

"No thanks," I said, smiling. "I need to touch base with Momma, anyway." I really had no plans to do so, but I didn't want to admit to Grace that I was just going to go home and be by myself until it was time for bed. It sounded pathetic even in my own mind.

"Are you sure? I feel guilty about leaving you out to dry with Jake out of town."

"Hey, you babysat me last night," I answered with a grin as I let her out at her house. "I'm good. No worries. Have a nice evening."

"You, too," she said. Before she closed the truck door, she said, "Call me if you need me, any time, day or night."

"Will do."

After Grace got inside, I turned the truck around and headed over to Momma's. Maybe I should call first. I'd popped in on them the day before without warning, and I didn't want to risk doing it two days in a row. "Momma, would you and Phillip care for a little company this evening?"

"We'd be delighted. In fact, I just took a chocolate cake out of the oven. In half an hour it will be ready to ice and eat."

"Count me in," I said with a laugh. It wasn't the pie I'd lied about earlier, and it wasn't taking place in Hickory, but cake in April Springs would be just as good, especially if it was one my mother made. She was more than just a land baron and mover and shaker in our little town; Momma was also one of the best cooks and bakers within a sixty-mile radius of home. The only reason I narrowed the distance was because of Napoli's. I would never dream of comparing the DeAngelis cooking with anyone else's, but if I had to eat a meal and I *wasn't* in Union Square, then Momma's table was where I wanted to be.

"Should I bring anything?" I asked. "The store should have milk again by now, since the roads are all clear."

"Thanks, but we're all set. All you need to do is bring yourself."

"That won't be a problem, since I take me with me wherever I go," I said, happy that I'd decided to pop in on her because of Jake's absence and Grace's date. "See you soon."

CHAPTER 12

"**W**OULD IT BE RUDE OF me to say that it looks as though Santa himself threw up in here?" I asked as Momma took my jacket at the door. There were even more decorations up than there had been just the day before. Sprigs of holly were everywhere, tinsel, garlands, stars, two trees now, and three manger scenes, one of them done completely in bears. "Those are new," I said as I pointed to the wise bears: Joseph Bear; Mary Bear; and Baby Jesus Bear.

"They were Phillip's choice," Momma said with a grin.

"You know what? Knowing that makes me like the man just a little bit more than I did before," I admitted. It often amazed me that the former chief of police and I had gone from outright adversaries to allies over the years, and no one had been more surprised by the development than I'd been myself. It was sometimes hard to remember the bad old days when he'd been April Spring's chief of police and I'd been a neophyte sleuth. I'd gained quite a bit of experience over the years, but I didn't kid myself. He'd been a real cop, and all I would *ever* be was an amateur.

"Do you like them?" Phillip asked me with a grin. He'd been heavy when he'd been the police chief, but while courting my mother, he'd dropped a great deal of the excessive weight, and to my surprise, he'd somehow managed to keep most of it off, despite Momma's excellent cooking.

"I think they're great," I said. "They'd look perfect on our mantel at the cottage."

"Consider it done," he said with a laugh. "Now I know what I'm getting you for Christmas."

"You haven't gotten us anything yet?" I asked with a smile. "Nothing like putting things off until the last minute. There aren't that many shopping days left until Christmas."

"He likes the pressure," Momma said.

"You, on the other hand, have been finished since the first of October, haven't you?"

"There's nothing wrong with being prepared," she said.

"You didn't deny it though, did you?" I asked as I hugged her.

"Suzanne, you vex me sometimes."

"Momma, if I didn't, that would mean that I wasn't properly doing my job. Thanks for the invitation. Grace and I had lasagna at Napoli's for dinner, so cake will be the perfect topper to the evening."

"You ate at Napoli's?" Phillip asked, the envy clear in his voice. "You didn't happen to bring anything home in a doggy bag, did you?"

Momma swatted her husband affectionately. "You had more than your share of pot roast tonight, sir."

"I know, but just thinking about Angelica's lasagna makes my mouth water."

"Actually, the girls cooked today," I countered.

"I'm willing to bet that it was still delightful," Phillip answered.

"Oh, it was. I just wish there hadn't been a bit of a cloud hanging over the meal."

Momma looked concerned. "What's wrong, Suzanne? Are you worried about your husband? Has anything happened in the mountains?"

"No, Jake is fine. In fact, I'm willing to bet that he's excellent. He managed to get a message to me from a ham radio operator that he's having a sweet old time. The truth is that he probably hasn't even noticed that I'm not there with him."

"Oh, he's noticed. Trust me on that," Momma's husband said with a smile.

"Do you know something? That's one of the sweetest things you've ever said to me in your life," I said, and then I surprised Phillip by kissing his cheek.

"Well, I'd better get back to it," he said, clearly uncomfortable with my unexpected display of affection. The former chief of police went back to the dining room table, while I followed Momma into the kitchen.

"Does he ever miss being a cop?" I asked her after we were alone.

She seemed surprised by my question. "No, he was long past due to retire. That job takes a toll on a person, man or woman. It was time for him to get out. Why, is Jake getting antsy?"

"I think so, but whenever I bring up the idea of him starting his own private detective firm, he shoots it down every time."

"He just needs a little distance from his old job," Momma said. "Give him some time. He'll be fine."

"I hope you're right. I just can't help worrying about it sometimes."

"That I understand completely," she said as she felt the temperature of the cake with her palm. "I need to let this rest a little longer before I ice it. Would you mind asking Phillip what he's working on while we wait? He has no one else to share it with, and I'm afraid I don't have your taste for crime." She must have realized how that sounded, because she quickly added, "You know what I mean."

"In fact, I do," I replied. "You'll call us when it's iced and ready to eat though, won't you?"

Momma laughed heartily, a sound I loved dearly. "You know I will."

I joined Phillip in the dining room and looked at the clippings he had out on the table. "What's this? Did you find something interesting?"

"It's an actual bank robbery from the seventies, if you can believe it. They never caught the two men who did it or even got the slightest whiff of the money. I bet it's still somewhere in town, waiting for someone to stumble across it."

"Wouldn't the two men who stole it have spent it long ago?" I asked him, intrigued by the premise that there was still loot somewhere around.

"My theory is that they squabbled over the money after stashing it away for safekeeping, and they ended up getting rid of each other before they could spend a dime of it."

"That's kind of grim, isn't it?"

"Maybe, but these things have been known to work out that way sometimes." Phillip pushed the clips away and focused on me. "How's your investigation going into Greg Whitmore's murder?"

"What makes you think I'm digging into that?" I asked him, trying to keep my expression even.

He laughed with real gusto. "Suzanne, you found the man! Of course you're digging into what happened to him. Do you have any serious suspects yet? I mean besides Lori."

"You know her?" I asked him.

"Our paths have crossed a time or two in the past," he admitted. "I never imagined those two would ever split up. You just never know, do you?"

"No, you don't. You're right; she looks like a prime suspect. In fact, she already lied to us once, and she has no alibi for the time of the murder."

"That's right. I heard that Penny was working at the hospital during the storm," Phillip said, surprising me with his knowledge.

"Okay, you need to explain yourself, sir. One, how did you

know Lori was staying with Penny, and two, how could you possibly know that she was working at the hospital all night?"

"It's not all that mysterious. An old friend of mine overexerted himself and was in the hospital, so Penny was kind enough to keep me updated. She also happened to mention that Lori was staying with her. She worried about losing power, so it's no mystery as to how I knew any of it."

"What happened to your friend? Was he caught out in the storm?"

"No, as a matter of fact, he was with his thirty-year-old girlfriend," Phillip said.

"What is it about older men and younger women?" I asked a little too forcefully. "Why can't they be happy with women their own age?"

"Hey, your mother happens to be *older* than I am," he said in his own defense. "To be fair, it's not all of us, but to answer your question, I think they're trying to recapture their youth and how they used to feel before the world had a chance to beat them down. As for the younger women, some of them have father issues, but some like the stability an older man can provide."

"Well, you seem to have thought a lot about this particular topic," I said. "Should Momma be worried?"

"No, but I have a lot of time on my hands to think about lots of things. Now, tell me about your other suspects."

I knew that I could use an impartial opinion, so I went quickly through our list for him. "Calvin Trinket was his boss at the bank, and the two of them have been arguing a lot lately. Greg was seeing a younger woman named Gwen who also works at the bank, and she's got more than a little crazy in her. Then there's Greg's best friend, who happened to be dating Gwen when Greg swooped in and stole her from him."

"My, you've been busy," he said after whistling softly. "Who do you like for it?"

"The truth of the matter is that it depends on who I'm talking to at the time," I admitted. "If you would have asked me yesterday who might want to see Greg Whitmore dead, I would have been hard pressed to name anyone beyond the possibility of Lori. I'm sure that's who the chief is focusing on."

"You can't blame him for that. Usually, in these cases, the most obvious choice is often the right one."

"But sometimes it's not," I countered.

"True enough. What's your plan going forward from here?"

I shook my head. "We're still considering the possibilities."

"Well, keep digging. It sounds as though you're on the right track."

"Do you have any advice that's more specific than that?" I asked him, clearly startling him with my question.

He thought about it for nearly a full minute before he spoke. "Well, it sounds as though what you really need is more information. Alibis, or lack of them, would be nice."

"We tried to get them, but we were met with resistance at every turn."

"That's the trouble with not having a badge, though that doesn't necessarily mean that folks won't lie to you, anyway. If I were you, I'd go back to that bank tomorrow, since that's where the majority of your suspects are. Your mere presence might be enough to shake something loose." He leaned in and added in a softer voice, "Do me a favor. Don't tell your mother that I'm actually encouraging you to stir this particular pot."

"My lips are sealed," I said with a grin. It was good advice, and I meant to take it, at least if nothing else changed between now and when I closed the donut shop the next day.

"What are you two conspiring about in here?" Momma asked as she reentered the room.

"We were just wondering if we were ever going to get cake, or if it was all just an empty promise," I said with a smile.

Phillip took an exaggerated breath. "Oh, there's cake, all right. I'm just not entirely certain that we're getting any of it, at least tonight."

"Well, I was about to say that it's ready and plated if you two would like some, but I'm enjoying your comedy routine so much that it can wait until you're finished. You let me know."

"Oh, it's finished," I said as I stood, and Phillip joined me. "Right?"

"Right as rain," he said.

"You're sure?" Momma asked.

"Stop torturing us, woman," Phillip said with affection and put his arm easily around my mother's waist. I knew in my heart that the man was good for her, and if it couldn't be my late father there with us now, I was happy enough that it was him.

"Okay. I give up. Let's go get some cake."

"Now you're talking," he said with obvious glee. "Usually, I adhere to the policy of Ladies First, but this time I'm making an exception. It's every cake lover for himself tonight."

"Or herself," I said with a grin.

Momma laughed at us both. "What am I going to do with you two?"

"Keep us both, I hope," Phillip said with a grin.

"Of that there can be no doubt."

After we finished eating our delicious dessert, Phillip pushed back from the table and started clearing the plates.

"Leave those," Momma said. "I'll get them later."

He frowned at her as he said, "I'm sorry, but I can't do that. You baked for us, so the least I can do is clean up."

She laughed, stood, and then kissed him soundly. "As much as I appreciate the sentiment, Suzanne and I will be delighted to do it. It will give us a chance to chat."

"Far be it from me to come between a mother and daughter," he said with a smile. "As always, it was delightful, my love. Thank you."

"You're most welcome," she said, and then he went back to his clippings.

"I'm glad you two found each other," I said after he was gone.

Momma looked pleased to hear it. "You haven't always felt that way, have you?"

"What can I say? It took me some time to warm up to the man, but he's all right in my book."

"I'm happy to hear it. Now, would you like to wash, or dry?"

"I'll dry," I said. Ordinarily the dishes would just go in the dishwasher, but Momma had clearly felt like celebrating, putting out her good china and crystal stemware for our cake and milk. We'd all foregone coffee, opting for chilled milk instead. The dishes, as nice as they were, had to be hand washed and carefully dried before being put away, but I didn't mind. It would give Momma and me a chance to catch up, something I sorely missed since she'd moved out of the cottage we'd shared since my divorce from Max.

We chatted about a great many things, none of them earthshattering, both of us basking in the other's company. By the time we finished the dishes, I caught myself yawning more and more frequently. "Excuse me," I said. "It's not even my bedtime yet."

"Maybe not, but you've had a full day. You won't hurt my feelings if you go home. I'm willing to bet that Phillip is already asleep. We have completely different schedules."

"Is that ever a problem for you?" I asked. Jake and I had very similar sleep patterns on the days I wasn't working at the donut shop. We both rose early and faced the day together, and by the time I was ready to call it a day, so was he.

"Actually, it's a bit of a blessing. This way he has some personal time in the morning while I have some at night. None of my businesses require constant attention, so we still have quite a bit of free time together over the course of the day. I'd highly recommend it. You'll see for yourself when you retire."

"You're kidding, right? I'm never leaving the donut shop," I said with a smile. "I'd like to make my last batch of donuts and then keel over on the spot."

"What a grim image that conjures up," Momma said with a smile.

"Haven't you ever thought about how you'd like to go?" I asked her.

"I'm not exactly certain how we got on this topic, because I certainly don't spend any time thinking about it. I imagine I'll be ready to go once everything I've set out to accomplish has been achieved."

"At the ripe old age of one hundred twenty-three, right?" I asked her.

"No, I imagine I'll be ready to wrap things up sometime before triple digits roll around." She took the drying rag from me and put it on the oven handle bar, allowing it to dry naturally. "I've redecorated the guest room since you've seen it. Let me show you."

"Okay, but then I really need to get home."

"Fine, if that's what you'd really like to do, but you know you're more than welcome to stay here with us tonight."

I just shrugged, not really knowing how to respond to her offer. Part of me was tempted, since Jake was away, but another part reminded me that I was a grown woman, perfectly capable of staying in my own cottage alone at night.

I followed Momma out into the dining room and into the

main living space. Phillip was nowhere to be found, and I had to assume that he'd already gone off to bed. I followed Momma down the hallway into the guest room, and as she opened the door, she flipped on the overhead light.

She hadn't been exaggerating. One wall of the room had been replaced with weathered barn boards, there was a rustic wooden floor instead of the carpet that had been there before, and the bed looked big enough to accommodate at least four adults, though I could never imagine the circumstances that particular trait might be needed. The central ceiling light was a chandelier made of driftwood, though we were quite a few miles from the nearest ocean beach. "Wow, it's really rustic, isn't it?"

"I got the idea from one of the design shows on television," she said. "The floor's not really wood, though. It's tile."

I found that hard to believe until I knelt down for a closer look. Sure enough, though there was a pattern of weathered gray wood on each piece, it was indeed tile. Something struck me as odd, though. My hand felt warm.

"Did you put radiant floor heat in here?" I asked her.

"We did it in both bedrooms," she admitted. "It gives the tiles such a cozy feel when you step on them in the morning."

"I can't wait to see the bathroom," I said. Though Momma's cottage offered only two bedrooms, each was its own master suite. In fact, there were more bathrooms than bedrooms in the place, something that had always struck me as odd.

"Don't get your hopes up. I haven't had a chance to modify that yet."

Sure enough, the bathroom was as I had seen it before, with tumbled tiles on the floor, a granite countertop for the sink, and a walk-in shower with a massive wall of glass. "This is nothing to be ashamed of. It's still really nice."

"I suppose, but just wait until you see what I have planned

for it," she said with a grin. "Suzanne, why don't you stay? I'd love to have you."

"I won't be much company," I reminded her. "As you pointed out earlier, it's almost time for bed."

"I can't explain it, but as a mother, it would be nice just knowing that we were under the same roof again, if only for one night."

The wistful tone in her voice told me that it was more important to her that I stay than for me to assert my independence. "Okay. Thanks. I'd love to."

"That's delightful," she said gleefully, telling me that I'd made the right decision.

"There's just one problem, though," I said. "I don't have anything to sleep in."

Momma grinned. "That's what you think. Look in the top drawer of the dresser."

Before I checked to see what she was talking about, I noticed a single framed photograph on top. I recognized it instantly. It had been taken one Christmas morning when I'd been a child. I was opening up a tall toy kitchen while Momma and Dad beamed at me. It was one of those rare photos with my dad actually in it, since he was usually the family photographer. He must have put this one on a timer, and he'd managed to capture the moment perfectly. I stroked the image of him lightly, and then I smiled at Momma. "This is sweet."

"I like to remind myself of those carefree times, especially when you're vexing me," she added with a grin.

"Wow, this photo must get a real workout, if that's the case," I replied happily.

"Go on. Look in the drawer."

"Yes, ma'am," I said as I pulled the drawer in question out and was surprised to see not only a nightgown there but a complete change of clothes as well: jeans, T-shirt, undies, and socks. As I picked the jeans up, I said, "These are my size."

"Don't you think I knew that?" she asked me.

"I'm confused. *I* didn't even know I was staying here until thirty seconds ago. How could you have possibly known?"

"Suzanne, I've kept a change of clothes for you here ever since Phillip and I moved in."

"You weren't expecting Jake and me to have problems, were you?"

"Of course not," she said hastily. "I wanted to be prepared, just in case. Check the second drawer."

I did as she'd instructed and was even more surprised to find a set of man's pajamas there, as well as a complete outfit for my husband. I didn't even have to see the size to know that they were spot on as well. "Momma, I thought I liked to overprepare, but you put me to shame. You know that, don't you?"

"It never hurts to be ready for the unexpected," she said. "There are towels in the linen closet, and I've got those little shampoos and soap in the bathroom as well."

"Momma, you haven't been stealing them from hotel rooms, have you?" I asked her with a smile.

She shook her head. "You realize that you can buy them in the store as well."

"Sure, but what fun is that?" I asked as I gave her a hug. "Thanks for thinking of everything."

"If only I could," she said, returning my hug in full. "The sheer number of events I have no contingency plans for keeps me up some nights. I do what I can, but is it ever enough? I'm afraid that the only way I'll ever find out is to experience the emergency and fail to have prepared adequately for it."

"On that bright note, I'm going to bed now," I said with a grin.

"Sleep well."

"I'll try not to wake you in the middle of the night when I leave," I said as she headed for the door.

She nodded and left, and soon I was alone. I wanted to call Jake, but I knew there was no way a signal could get through to him. I'd have to be satisfied with the message I'd received earlier and leave it at that, but it still would have been nice to hear his voice before I drifted off to sleep. I had a tough time getting to sleep, so I grabbed the book club selection from my bag and finished the book before finally nodding off.

CHAPTER 13

I DIDN'T EVEN NEED AN ALARM clock to wake me the next
morning, I was so used to getting up at a certain time.
I'd forgotten all about the heated floors until my bare
feet hit the tiles. Wow, that was nice! Jake and I were going to
have to look into retrofitting our own cottage with it, though
I imagined it would be more expensive than our budget could
stand, especially with the repair and remodeling of the donut
shop looming in our not-too-distant future. I figured insurance
would take care of most of the bill, but if experience had taught
me anything, it was that other expenses would arise that weren't
covered by my policy. I took a quick shower, changed into the
clothes Momma had purchased for me, and I was relieved to see
that they fit, albeit a little snugly. *Suzanne, you really need to cut
back on sampling your own goodies!*

Slowly opening the bedroom door, I tiptoed out into the
living room and saw a light on in the kitchen. Did Momma and
Phillip leave one on at night to serve as a nightlight, or had it
been left on to aid me in getting around the unfamiliar space? I
walked into the kitchen to shut it off only to find Momma up,
standing over a pan containing eggs and bacon. The smell of
fresh coffee welcomed me as well. How had I not smelled all of
that in my bedroom?

"Did you get up just to make me breakfast?" I asked her after
giving her a brief hug.

"Well, I'm certainly not eating this early, unless you want

the company. I've got toast for you, too." As she said it, the toaster popped up as though on cue.

"I usually don't eat much in the mornings before I go to work," I admitted.

"Well, let today be the exception, then. If you don't eat it, I'll have to wake Phillip up so he can, and he'll never get back to sleep if he eats all of this. What do you say? It's entirely up to you. Are you going to have this yourself, or do we need to rouse my husband?"

I had to laugh. Parts of my mother's personality had changed over the years, but other parts were still there in full force. "I give up. I'll eat," I said as I took a seat.

"Good girl," Momma said as she plated up my food and slid it in front of me.

"This is really delicious," I said after digging in. I would have never gone to so much trouble for myself, but who was I to turn down my mother's offerings?

Momma sat at the table with me as I ate, and after I finished, she said, "Suzanne, there's something I'd like to discuss with you before you go."

Uh oh. What was going on here? "What's wrong? Am I in trouble?"

Momma laughed heartily at the face I must have been making. "Of course not. I just wanted to discuss Greg Whitmore's murder with you."

"Did Phillip tell you that Grace and I were looking into it?" I asked, wondering why my stepfather had decided to share that information with her.

"No, he would never violate a confidence," she said. "It just so happens that I was eavesdropping on your conversation last night from the kitchen."

I couldn't even be angry with her. After all, it was definitely a case of the apple not falling far from the tree. If our roles had been reversed, we both knew that my ear would have been at that door before it could even fully close. "What do you think?"

"Phillip has some good advice, but you might need a little more leverage to get anyone to talk to you at the bank a second time." Momma reached over to the counter and grabbed a piece of paper. It was a check, and when I saw the amount, I realized that it was more money than I cleared in a year at the donut shop.

"Wow, if this is my allowance, I'm moving back in immediately," I told her with a smile.

"Don't be silly. You're to take this to the bank this afternoon to prove that your questions deserve to be answered. It's amazing what a little money and the promise of spreading it around can do for a situation like you're in."

"Is it good?" I asked her as I waved the check in the air.

"Of course it's good. I would never write a bad check, even for something like this."

I took a deep breath and treated the check a little more reverently. "I know you don't like to discuss business with me, but is there any reason in particular that you have one hundred thousand dollars in your checking account?"

Momma smiled. "I'm buying a piece of property tomorrow, so you just happened to catch me at the perfect time. If anyone at the bank checks this, they'll find that it's perfectly good. Anyway, perhaps it will help."

I studied the check, which was made out to cash, and noticed that something was missing. I handed it back to her and said, "You forgot to sign it."

She laughed. "Oh, how I miss you. I certainly didn't forget to do anything. You are to use this as leverage, but not actually deposit it. Do we understand each other? This represents good faith on your part, which happens to be completely lacking, but so be it. If it helps you find the man's killer, then I'm willing to participate in the ruse."

"I didn't realize you cared so much about Greg Whitmore," I said.

"I barely knew the man. I'm not doing this for him, Suzanne. It's for you. I understand why you and Grace feel the need to investigate his murder, since you were the ones who found his body. I'm not sure I wouldn't do the same thing were I in your shoes instead."

"Thank you, Momma. I appreciate this," I said as I folded the check and stuck it in my front pocket. "I won't let you down."

"You couldn't even if you tried," she said. "Now, don't you have a donut shop to go to?"

I glanced at the clock and saw that I was indeed running behind schedule, which was only fair, since I hadn't planned on stopping for such a lavish breakfast. "I'll still make it. After all, even if I'm a little late, who's going to complain? There are real benefits of being the boss, and I know that I don't have to tell you that."

"You do not." As I got up to leave, Momma added, "Suzanne, you know you're more than welcome to stay here with us again tonight."

"I know, and I appreciate it."

"So, does that mean we can count on you?" she asked.

"Let's just play it by ear for now, okay?" I replied.

"That's fine. Have a lovely day."

"You, too," I said.

She yawned once and then nodded. "I plan to, but it's going to start quite a bit later than yours has. I'm going back to bed."

"You didn't have to get up just for me," I reminded her.

"I'd rather lose a little sleep than some time with my favorite daughter," she said as she kissed my cheek.

"It probably helps that I'm your *only* daughter," I said, laughing.

"That it does."

I drove to the donut shop in the darkness and realized that the streets weren't completely free from complications. Most of the moisture had dried off in the sunlight, but there were still patches of black ice hiding in the shade of some tall trees that nearly made me lose control of Jake's truck a couple of times. It wasn't exactly a pristine vehicle, but if I put any new dents or scrapes on it, my husband would realize it instantly. Fortunately, I made it to Donut Hearts unscathed. The front of the shop looked as though it had a black eye with the hastily patched roof and corner walls, and I knew that I'd have to fix it sooner rather than later. I couldn't expect my customers to put up with folding seats when they'd been used to comfortable couches and upholstered chairs. That was when I remembered the book club meeting scheduled for that morning. Should I cancel, or should we just go ahead with it? I knew the ladies would rather put up with the hardship of folding chairs than they would with skipping a meeting, so I decided to let them decide once they got there. At least I'd finished the book, and I had a few questions for the group.

That would have to wait until later, though.

Right now I had donuts to make.

As I began to gather supplies, I was happy seeing that my pantry was fully restocked, and I was even ready to face another storm if need be.

But I hoped with all my heart that it wouldn't come. I wouldn't mind a white Christmas, but I was already thoroughly tired of ice.

Emma came in happier than usual, especially for that time of night. "Good morning, Suzanne," she said as I started dropping pumpkin cake donuts into the oil. "Oops. I'll be out front if you need me." She quickly stepped back out into the dining area, and I finished up the last of the cake donuts, icing them and setting them on racks to one side so they could cool completely.

"You can come in now," I said as I walked through the door that separated the kitchen from the display and dining area.

"Look what I brought you," she said as she held a copy of the *April Springs Sentinel* up for me to see. "It's hot off the presses."

I took the paper from her and read the banner headline, "*ICE CRIPPLES TOWN.*" "Your father isn't afraid of using ink, is he?"

"Are you kidding? He's in heaven. He spent all day yesterday going around taking pictures and interviewing folks about the Great Ice Storm of the Century. That's what he's been calling it. You can almost hear the capital letters in his voice."

"Is there anything here about Greg Whitmore?" I asked her, trying to be as nonchalant about it as I could. I didn't want her father to know just yet what Grace and I were up to, so it made sense to keep it from Emma, too, at least for the moment.

"Check the black box below the fold," she instructed me.

I read Ray Blake's brief aside aloud.

"'*SANTA SLAYING IN THE PARK! The storm did more than strike terror in the hearts of April Springs residents. Greg Whitmore, aged 58, perished during the storm, cut down in cold blood in his prime. For more on this story, see tomorrow's special edition, Killer Storm.*' Wow, he really knows how to sell the next newspaper, doesn't he? I'm not so sure about fifty-eight being someone's prime, but then again, I used to think thirty was old when I was a kid."

"I still do," Emma said with a grin.

"Just wait ten years and you'll know exactly what I mean."

"Dad's upset about Greg's murder, but the storm has been a

real blessing. He's printing twice the number of copies as usual. He thinks this one is going to be a collector's edition."

"He could be right at that," I said. "What does he think about what happened to Greg?"

"You know Dad. He's got a dozen theories, each one wilder than the last."

I looked hard at my assistant, who was still smiling broadly. "Is that why you're so happy, because your dad is selling papers?"

"I'm not supposed to say anything until it's official, but it looks like Barton is staying in town after all."

Barton Gleason was the new chef at the hospital, a culinary magician who was all set to leave town for a job in Charlotte before Emma came into his life. I was a fan of the man, both for who he was and for the art of what he did in the kitchen. "That's great news."

"You're telling me," she said. "Can I tell you something?"

"I sure hope so," I said, smiling.

"Suzanne, he might be the one." Emma bit her lip, and before I could say anything, she quickly added, "I know I've said that before, but this time I think there's a chance that it just might be true."

"Good for you," I said. "Now, why don't you tell me all about it while you get started on those dishes and I get the yeast dough ready for its first rise?"

"I thought you'd never ask," Emma said. As she chattered away happily about her new love, I had to smile to myself. My assistant and dear friend had fallen in love at least half a dozen times since she'd come to work for me at Donut Hearts, but I had a feeling that maybe this time, it would be for keeps. I myself was a true believer in love, especially after finding Jake, but I'd made a promise to myself not to meddle in Emma's love life, well, at least not as much as I had in the past, and so far, I'd done a pretty good job of sticking to it.

That didn't mean that I couldn't be happy for her, though.

By the time we were ready for our break outside, I had the yeast dough ready, and Emma had knocked out enough of the dirty dishes for the next phase of our work. "We're going outside, aren't we?" she asked me eagerly. "I know the tables and chairs out there are gone, along with the awning, but we can drag a pair of folding chairs out with us, can't we?"

"There's no reason we shouldn't," I said. I didn't mind the cold, but I missed my things, and every time I stepped out into the dining area, I realized how much of the place I'd lost.

Emma must have sensed my mood. "Come on, Suzanne. The brisk air will do you good. Don't worry about all of this," she said as she waved a hand around in the front of the shop. "It will be as good as new again before you know it."

"I hope so," I said.

Emma was right, at least about the cold. I loved the chilly embrace of this time of year. It was a nice juxtaposition to the heat coming off the hot oil inside, and there was a freshness to the air that with every breath, it felt as though I were experiencing it for the first time. That being said, I was still happy when the timer went off and it was time to go back inside. Cold was good if it was easy to transition back to warm, and I never took that luxury for granted.

CHAPTER 14

"GWEN, WHAT ARE YOU DOING here?" I asked Greg's former girlfriend as I unlocked the front door the moment it was time to open for the day and start selling what I'd been so carefully creating all morning.

"I need to talk to you," she said urgently as I let her in. Gwen was my first customer of the day, and no one else was waiting for my donuts. I couldn't blame them. It was chilly out, and I knew that my regulars would be along soon enough.

"I'm all yours," I said.

"Listen, I need to straighten you out about something," she said as she frowned.

"I didn't even realize that I was bent," I said, doing my best not to react to her comment.

"That's not what I mean. I'm talking about Greg."

"What about him?" I asked. "By the way, can I get you anything while you're here?"

She frowned at my donut display, shook her head, and then said, "Just coffee."

It wasn't that I didn't trust people who didn't like donuts; well, maybe that *was* it. The woman had another strike against her, and they were piling up fast. I poured her coffee, took her money, and then handed her change to her. "You were saying?" I asked after the transaction was completed.

"There's a great deal more going on here than you're aware

of, and if you don't be careful, it's going to cost you something dear to you."

"Is that a threat, Gwen?" I asked her, letting a little of the tenseness I was feeling out in my voice.

"What? Of course not. I came to warn you! Do you think I'd drive all the way here at this unholy hour just to threaten you? Suzanne, there are things going on behind the scenes that, if you stumble into them, could hurt you."

"For example?"

She shrugged. "Okay. Here's a big one. Why do you think Greg was really in the hospital a while back?"

"That's an easy one. He was in a car accident," I said, remembering how Lori had come and bought out my inventory so her husband could have all the treats he wanted upon being discharged.

"That's just what he wanted people to think," she said smugly.

"Are you saying that's not what happened?"

"A blow from a baseball bat to the ribs isn't that unlike a car wreck," Gwen said.

I narrowed my gaze. "Greg was beaten? If that were true, then why would he lie about it?"

"Because he was promised a great deal worse than that if he didn't cooperate." Gwen kept looking over her shoulder out the Plexiglas window, and I was beginning to understand why. I believed that she was genuinely afraid. What I didn't know was if there was any basis for her fear in reality.

"Okay, let's say I believe you. Who would do such a thing?"

"My boss," she said softly, as though Calvin Trinket could actually hear her.

"Let me get this straight. You're trying to tell me that Calvin hit Greg with a baseball bat," I said. It was ridiculous thinking of that older, heavyset man attacking Greg so overtly.

"Calvin didn't do the actual deed," she said in disgust, "but he was the direct cause of it."

"I'm listening," I said, fighting to keep an open mind.

"This is where it gets complicated," Gwen said. "I didn't tell you the complete story earlier because I didn't want to burden you with it, but you need to know. A while back, I found out that Calvin forced Greg into making some bad loans, and when Greg realized what was going on, he threatened to go to the authorities. After his 'accident,' he quit complaining so openly about it, until this past week, that is. I urged him to go to the police, and he was starting to come around to my way of thinking. Calvin couldn't have that, so I'm thinking he told his partners what was going on, and they took things a little too far trying to scare Greg into complying with their wishes."

"Why wouldn't Calvin issue the loans himself? Why would he even involve Greg?" I asked, and then I realized what the answer was. "He wanted plausible deniability that he even knew what was going on, didn't he?"

"Exactly. I told you Calvin and Greg had been fighting recently, and that was the real reason why. Greg is in fear for his life, and suddenly he turns up dead. He and Calvin are fighting. You do the math."

I thought it was still a bit of a leap, even if everything she'd just told me was true. "Wouldn't killing Greg just serve to put the spotlight on the loans he'd issued?" I asked. "I'd think they wouldn't want any attention at all."

"That's why I said things must have gotten out of hand," Gwen said after sipping her coffee.

"Who exactly *are* these people?" I asked her. I needed something to take to the police chief, something more substantial than Gwen's story so far.

"I don't know," she said, glancing back once again over her shoulder.

"You don't know, or you won't say?" I asked her.

"Suzanne, I'm already in enough danger as it is without blabbing more of it to you."

"I get that," I said as I saw a few customers approaching. "The real question is, why are you really here if you truly are putting your own life at risk?"

"I couldn't just see you walk into this blindly." She glanced back again and saw the men approaching. "I've got to go."

"Relax, they're regulars here," I said, doing my best to reassure her.

It didn't work.

"No thank you. I'm getting out of town," she said, "and I'm not coming back until this thing is resolved, one way or another."

"What about your job?"

"It's not worth more than my life to me. Besides, I was looking for this one when I found it, so I'm sure I'll be able to find something else without too much trouble. I've got some vacation time saved up that I'm about to take on the spur of the moment, and if I run out of that, then I'll find something else to do. No job is worth dying over, certainly not mine."

"Suzanne, it's colder than a well-digger's nose out there right now," Ashton Sinclair said as he rubbed his hands together after stepping into the donut shop.

"I'll be with you in a second," I said, and then I turned back to Gwen, but she was already on her way out the door.

"Sorry if I scared her off," Ashton said with a grin. "I seem to have that effect on young women."

"Old ones, too," Jefferson Branch said as he joined his old friend.

"True enough," Ashton replied with a smile.

As they ordered donuts and coffee, I wondered what had sparked Gwen's self-professed humanitarian act coming to warn me that I might be in danger. Had she been telling the truth, or was it all a ruse to get me to drop my investigation into her relationship with Greg? It would be nice to verify her story, but the only person I knew I could ask was Benny Young. Hopefully he'd be at the bank later when Grace and I made our way back there with Momma's check. Either way, Gwen had just taken herself out of the mix of folks we could interview by leaving town. I decided as soon as I finished filling the men's orders, I needed to call Chief Grant and update him about what had just happened.

"Hey, it's Suzanne," I said when he picked up.

"How's my favorite donut maker in the world?" he asked me. The man was in a good mood, but I didn't have time to stop and ask him why.

"Thanks, but I'm probably the only donut maker in the world you know, so I'll take that with a grain of salt. Gwen West just came by the donut shop."

"Greg's girlfriend? She's a long way from home this early, isn't she?"

"She's about to be a great deal farther," I said. I repeated our conversation, and the chief hesitated before answering. "How long ago did she leave?" he asked me.

"Two minutes," I said.

"It's a shame you didn't call me while she was still there," he said.

"I had a hunch she wouldn't just stand around here waiting for you. Do you believe her, Chief?"

"Let's just say that I have no reason not to believe her at this point," he said. "I spoke with her yesterday, and she didn't say a word about any of this to me then."

"Don't feel like the Lone Ranger. She's just coming clean with me now as well."

"Be that as it may, I'll look into it. Thanks for calling."

"You bet," I said. "I'm just trying to keep up my end of the bargain."

"I appreciate that. Listen, I've got to go," he said, and then he hung up on me abruptly.

I wondered what had pulled him away so suddenly. There was no way to know, since he hadn't felt like sharing, so I did what I do best: I got back to selling donuts and coffee, with a little hot chocolate thrown in every now and then. For the moment, Gwen was Chief Grant's problem, along with the investigation into what had really happened to Greg Whitmore.

"Hey, Suzanne," Roy Olsen, my insurance man, said when he came into the donut shop a little later. Roy was a tall, willowy man ten years my senior, but at the moment, he looked old enough to be my father.

"Are you getting any sleep at all, Roy?" I asked him sympathetically.

"No, and not much prospect of any in the future." He surveyed the damage from the inside, and then he asked, "You've got pictures of all of this before anyone did any work, right?"

"Yes, they're on my phone," I said. "Hang on." I went back and got Emma, who was just finishing up a batch of dishes. "Can you catch the front for me for a few minutes? Roy Olsen is here."

"Absolutely," she said.

After Emma was at the helm, I joined Roy at the site of the worst damage we'd sustained. I pulled out my phone and started swiping through the photos. He nodded, stopped me a few times and had me back up, and then he smiled softly. "You'd be amazed at how many people don't document things at all before they start mucking them up."

I surveyed the hasty repairs my friends had done and did

my best not to take offense at his comment. "I don't know. For being done at the spur of the moment, I think they did a pretty good job."

"I didn't mean that how it must have sounded," he said apologetically. "Sorry. When I'm sleep deprived, I'm not the sweetest guy in the world. At least that's what my wife tells me." He looked around. "Where is the furniture?"

"George took it to City Hall to try to dry it, but it turns out that it's all ruined," I said. The mayor had left me a message on my machine that morning, and it hadn't done anything to help my mood starting off my workday. "I'm honestly more concerned about the building itself right now."

"No worries, we'll take care of as much of it as we can. I'll need three bids before you get the work done. Do you have anyone you'd like to use?"

"No one springs to mind," I said. I would have trusted the job to Tim Leander, but he was long gone.

"I'm sure your mother has someone good," he said absently. "Go on and get me those estimates, and I'll expedite things for you as much as I can."

"I appreciate that," I said, feeling sympathy for the man. The job was going to kill him if he didn't find a way to start taking it easy. "Can I get you something before you go? A donut or two? Maybe some coffee?"

He shuddered at the mention of coffee. "If I have another cup, I think I'll probably scream."

"Hot cocoa, then?"

"Sold. I wouldn't say no to a fritter, either."

"Luckily, you came to the right place," I said with a smile. After I set him up, he tried to pay, but I wouldn't let him. "No worries. It's on the house."

"I can't do that," he said as he counted out the money and

handed it to Emma, who took it after glancing at me and seeing me nod my head in agreement.

"Are you kidding? You should have come by yesterday. We were giving *everything* in the shop away after the ice storm. We couldn't make donuts fast enough."

Roy frowned. "You're not claiming any of that as a loss, are you?"

"No, sir, I'd never do that," I said, looking him steadily in the eye. "Momma paid for the supplies, and the labor and delivery services were both provided free of charge. We decided to help out our community in its time of need. We had no intention of making a profit because of other people's misery."

"I've done it again, haven't I?" Roy asked, feeling embarrassed about his earlier behavior. "Sorry again. I'm just tired."

"No worries. I won't tell anyone if you won't," I said with a smile. "Now, is there anything else I can do for you?"

"Please don't tell your mother how I behaved. If I lost her business, I'd have to shut the place down."

"We're all good, Roy."

"Would you mind forwarding those pictures to my number? I'll print them out and put them in your file."

"Happy to do it," I said as I performed the task before I forgot to do it later. It was a modern convenience that I was happy with, and I couldn't count the times I'd used my cell phone to take pictures of things I wanted to document. I thought about the pictures I'd taken of Greg in the park, and I knew that I needed to forward them to the police chief, but he had photos of his own, so there was no hurry. I needed to look over them again myself, since I now knew that Greg had been murdered instead of just freezing to death, but again, there just wasn't time at that moment.

Once Roy was gone, I stared at the repairs my friends had made for me. I knew that I'd have to get it all fixed, and sooner rather than later, but I had something far more important on my mind at the moment.

Once Greg's killer was caught and Jake was home again, I could focus on repairing my beloved donut shop.

In the meantime, the patches would just have to do.

After Roy left, I sent Emma back to the kitchen, and during a lull, I looked around at the folding chairs that made up my dining area. I would have to do something about that, since the roof was watertight again. The uniqueness of my current situation would wear off soon enough, and if I didn't, or couldn't, provide comfy places for my customers to sit and enjoy their treats, and soon, I was going to start losing business.

CHAPTER 15

"Suzanne, this place is tragic. Are we still having our book club meeting here today?" Jennifer asked me as she walked in with Hazel and Elizabeth close on her heels. The women were some of my best friends and the complete and sum total of our monthly book club group. They'd come into Donut Hearts once long ago to hold their meeting after their regular venue was unavailable, and they'd taken me in and made me feel special from the very start, even though their social and economic strata were miles and miles above mine.

"We can still have it, if you all don't mind sitting on folding chairs," I explained.

Jennifer looked at the chairs in question as the other ladies stood beside her, and then she frowned as she considered the only option available to us. With a voice heavy with sadness, she finally said, "I'm sorry, Suzanne, but this just won't do."

"Honestly, it's the best I have to offer, but I completely understand if you want to cancel this month's meeting," I said, apologizing as quickly as I could. "You see, we had an ice storm in town yesterday, and all of my furniture was ruined in the process."

"Stop teasing her, Jennifer," Hazel said, chiding our leader. "It's not nice."

"No, but it's fun," Elizabeth added with a smile.

"Well, I can tell you that it's not that fun for me," I said with a frown. They were usually so much nicer to me. What was going on here?

"Suzanne, I'm sorry. I was just trying to amuse you. The fact is that we heard about your plight yesterday afternoon," Jennifer explained.

"How could you have possibly heard about what happened here that quickly?"

"Let's just say that a little bird told us and leave it at that," the book club leader said with a smile.

I had a hunch the little bird in question was washing dishes in back, and I was going to have a word with her later, after everyone was gone. "Like I said, I'm sorry about the arrangements. If you all want to cancel, I completely get it."

"Jennifer, you need to tell them to come in right now, or I will," Hazel insisted. "This has gone on far enough."

"You're right," she said as she waved a hand out the door and called out, "Let's go."

"Who exactly are you inviting in?" I asked her, but no one would answer my question.

The three women began gathering the folding chairs up and setting them off to one side as the front door opened and four burly men came in carrying two large couches between them. The sofas were absolutely lovely, and I knew in an instant they each cost more than I could ever hope to afford, even with my insurance settlement that I wasn't going to get anytime soon. "What's going on?"

Jennifer explained, "My husband just bought another new company in Hickory that makes furniture. When we heard about your dilemma, I asked him for anything he had on hand that might be out of date, or patterns that didn't work; I was basically asking for anything I could give to you."

"Wow, you make it sound so sweet and thoughtful when you put it that way," Elizabeth said sarcastically.

"I'm not handling this very well, am I?" she asked. "It's all much better than I've represented it. I went through his inventory and pulled out some things I thought you might like, and voila, here they are."

I ran my hand over one of the couches, amazed by the softness of the fabric. "Jennifer, it's a lovely gesture, but even with a steep discount, I'm sure I can't afford these. I appreciate the thought, though."

"Dear woman, these are a gift, as well as the four chairs that are on their way too, or will be as soon as someone goes to fetch them as well." She glanced at the men, who got the message and left hastily to retrieve the rest of the furniture.

"I really couldn't accept," I said, stunned by her generosity.

"Don't worry about it; we all chipped in," Hazel said.

"If you're dead set on refusing them as gifts, you can always pay us back by providing the treats whenever we meet," Elizabeth offered.

"Exactly how long do you expect our club is going to be getting together?" I asked her with a grin.

"Long enough to make this a solid investment on our part. Please accept these items as tokens of our friendship and appreciation," Jennifer said with a warm smile.

"I don't know what to say," I said in one of those rare moments that I was actually struggling to find words to express the depth of my emotions.

"Just say thank you," Hazel suggested softly.

"Thank you," I said, echoing her sentiment.

"You're so very welcome," Jennifer said. After the chairs were delivered, she looked them over and said, "There. That is so much better than folding chairs."

"It's nicer than the furniture that's in my house. I still can't believe you all did this," I said, sitting down on one of the chairs for a moment and feeling its gentle embrace. It was so comfortable that I wasn't sure I was ever going to get up again.

"That's more than enough thanks," Jennifer said matter-of-factly. "Now, are you ladies ready for our Secret Santa exchange?"

"I know I am," I said. I'd had the gift I'd gotten for Elizabeth wrapped and at the front counter for several days, waiting for the moment I could give it to her. Thank goodness it hadn't been damaged when the tree had crashed into Donut Hearts.

"There's just one thing missing," Jennifer said as she looked around the room again, and at that moment, the door opened once more as two of the men carried in a fully decorated Christmas tree. They set it up in the corner where the tree had hit the building the day before, virtually blocking my view of most of the damage to my structure. As one of the movers plugged the lights in, I was so touched by the gesture that I began to tear up. The others graciously pretended not to notice, and as I wiped the tears away, Emma came out, saw what was going on, and immediately tried to turn on her heel and leave.

"Not so fast, young lady," I said as I walked toward her.

"Before you say anything, just know that I was..."

I stopped her from explaining or apologizing by embracing her with a hearty hug. "Thank you," I whispered in her ear.

"You're very welcome," she said, clearly relieved that I'd forgiven her breach of etiquette by contacting the book club ladies without my permission.

"Now, if you'll take the register, we have business to carry on," I said as I winked at her.

"I'm more than happy to do it," she said. "Here's the present you've been saving."

I took it from her and handed it to Elizabeth.

"What's this?" she asked as she began to unwrap it.

"You tell me," I said as I watched her rip into the paper like an excited child.

Elizabeth looked at it, read the cover, and then started leafing through the pages, squealing with delight the entire time.

"Where did you get this?" she asked, clasping it to her chest as though it were her most cherished possession.

"I found it on eBay. Don't worry, I stayed within our ten-dollar limit, though just barely."

"Don't hog it, Elizabeth. What is it?" Hazel asked.

"It's the Mystery International Group's email list," she said with a grin. "I thought it was a myth, and I never dreamed that even if it did exist, I'd ever have my very own copy."

"You'll have to tell us a little more than that," Jennifer said.

"This booklet contains the email addresses of nearly all of my favorite mystery writers. You all know how I love to correspond with the people who bring such joy to my life. I can't believe this is mine."

"It sounds a bit invasive, doesn't it?" Jennifer asked me with a slight grimace. "What if those addresses were meant to be private?"

"That's the beauty of it," I explained. "This particular list is made up entirely of writers who are open to hearing from their readers. It was a special printing, and I happened to be lucky enough to find one."

"It's magic, magic I tell you," Elizabeth said, still holding onto it as though it were her only tie to land in a stormy sea. "I feel bad about what I got Hazel now."

"What is it?" Hazel asked, reaching for the small box with a ribbon on top. When she opened it up, her face lit up. "I don't believe it. It's an Emperor Brownie," she said in a hushed tone.

"What exactly is that?" I asked her.

"They only make them twice a year, and you have to get on the waiting list at least twelve months in advance to have any hope of getting one."

"That's about how long it took, too," Elizabeth said with a grin. "When we drew names last year and I got yours, I put my name in the hat immediately, and sure enough, we got lucky this year."

"You are amazing," Hazel said, carefully closing the box again, "though you did go over the limit."

"Sorry about that," Elizabeth replied, with no remorse at all.

"Don't we all get a taste of it?" Jennifer asked as she studied the box in Hazel's hands.

"Yes. Of course," she said. The reluctance was heavy in her voice, but it was clear that she was still willing to share.

"Why does no one get it when I'm joking?" Jennifer asked us, clearly frustrated by our failure to get her humor. "I was just teasing."

"I really don't mind sharing," Hazel insisted.

"Nonsense," Jennifer said as she tried to hand something to me, but I shook my head.

"There is no way I can accept anything else from you."

"That was from all of us. This is from just me," she said.

I looked at the present in her hand reluctantly, but I didn't want to insult her by refusing her gift. I unwrapped the small box and found a heart-shaped pendant inside, decorated with hand-painted icing and sprinkles. "I know it's silly," Jennifer said, "but it's a donut heart. I found it at a quaint little shop in Charlotte, and I knew I had to get it for you."

"It's wonderful," I said as I put it on. "It's absolutely perfect."

We finished exchanging gifts, and then it was time to get down to business. After I got everyone coffee and donuts, we settled down on my new furniture and started our discussion.

"This book was a tough one for me," Hazel said. "I wanted to like it, but I kept thinking that I'd read it somewhere before."

"That's my fault," Jennifer answered contritely. "I chose the book thinking that it sounded interesting, but it wasn't until long after I read it that I realized how similarly it mirrored the first *Country Cooks* mystery."

"That's it!" Elizabeth said. "I knew it felt familiar to me, but I'd just assumed that I'd already read it and forgotten it. Why, the author didn't even bother changing the original name of the protagonist all that much! She went from Ellie to Ellen, and even her best friend's name was close to being the same. Not only that, but the subplot of the original book was eerily similar as well."

"I read once that you can't copyright a title, a subject, or even a storyline," I said, "but I still felt a little cheated by the echoed plot."

"I completely agree," Hazel said.

"At least we still have the original," I said. "I have an idea. Why don't we read *Cooking Up Trouble* next month? This imitation made me crave the original. What do you say to that?"

"I think it's a splendid idea," Jennifer said. "I'm afraid we're out of time anyway. The furniture and the Secret Santas took up more time than I thought they would. I wish for each and every one of you a very Merry Christmas."

We hugged each other in turn, and I asked Jennifer to stay behind as the other women left. "I don't know how to thank you. Please tell your husband that as long as I'm open, he can have as many donuts on the house as he'd like for the rest of his life."

"I would, but I'd be afraid he'd take you up on your offer, and he's fighting a losing battle with his waistline as it is," she said with a smile. "Honestly, this wasn't that big a deal, Suzanne."

"For me, it was epic. Thank you."

"You are very welcome. Now I'd better catch up with the others. Hazel is my ride, and I'd hate for her to leave me behind again."

Once they were gone, I marveled at how my shop had changed so completely for the better because of the generosity and friendship of the people in my life. I didn't have a lot of money, but I had friends that were worth more than gold to me, and as far as I was concerned, that made me richer than anyone else I'd ever known.

CHAPTER 16

"Lori, what are you doing here?" I asked Greg Whitmore's widow a few minutes before we were set to close for the day.

"I thought a donut might be nice," she said as she looked over my meager supply of treats left. "Do you have any pumpkin ones?"

"Sorry. How about an apple cider donut? They're quite nice."

"I suppose it will do. How about cocoa?"

"No, it's gone as well. I have coffee, though."

She looked displeased that I was continuing to thwart her wishes, but hey, she couldn't expect me to have a full selection that late in my morning. "Whatever."

I set her up, and she glanced at my new furniture. "I heard a rumor that your furniture was all ruined."

"The old things were," I said. "My friends brought me all of this a little bit earlier."

"You must have some very nice friends," she said as she admired the new pieces.

"I do," I replied. Since there was no one else in the donut shop, I decided to push my luck a little with her. "Was there any other reason you came by besides a treat?"

"Yes. No. I'm not sure," she said in stilted succession.

"Well, I'm sure that *one* of those is the right answer," I answered with a grin. "I'm just not sure which one."

"There's something I need to tell you. Two things, actually."

I put the dishcloth in my hand down and gave her my full attention. "Go on. I'm listening."

After taking a deep breath, she said, "I'm sorry I lied to you yesterday."

"You lied?" I asked, trying not to give away that I knew exactly what she was talking about.

"I knew my husband had a girlfriend. Her name is Gwen West. Suzanne, I was humiliated. She's at least twenty-five years younger than I am. He made me look like a fool dating a child like that."

"Nobody would ever think less of you because of that," I said, and I meant it. It had happened to a few friends of mine in the past, being thrown away like litter for newer, younger versions of themselves. "If anyone were judged harshly by the situation, it would have been Greg."

"It wasn't entirely his fault. He didn't quite know what he was getting himself into when she set her sights on him," she said, apologizing for the man even after he was gone. "Gwen knew exactly the right buttons to push, and he never had a chance."

"Lori, did she break up your marriage, or did they start dating after it was over between the two of you?" I asked. The timing of it all could have played a role in Greg's murder, and even though I wasn't a fan of everything the man had done in his life, that didn't mean that I couldn't keep trying to find out who had killed him.

"I don't know," she said with a soft wail in her voice. I saw the kitchen door open slowly, and Emma slowly peeked out. It didn't take her long to retreat into the kitchen, and I didn't blame her. This situation was on its way downhill, and fast.

I remembered what Gwen had told me that morning about Greg's business practices. This was a good time to distract her with a different line of questioning. "Lori, would Greg have ever written any bad loans, say something that was on the edge of being illegal, by any chance?"

"No! Never!"

"You seem sure of yourself," I said. "How can you be so positive?"

"It wasn't that Greg was particularly high minded or anything," she said with a frown as she explained. "But we talked about it on more than one occasion. My late husband was deathly afraid of being locked up. Terrified, actually. There is no way he'd risk going to jail under any circumstances, so whoever told you he did anything the least bit shady was lying to you."

It was interesting how the two women in Greg's life had such diverse opinions of the man and what he was capable of. I wondered which one of them had known the real Greg Whitmore. "You said there were two things you wanted to talk about," I reminded her, hoping to head off a crying jag, no matter how deserved it might be.

"I did, but I can't quite bring myself to share that with you just yet."

"Come on. You know that you'll feel better once you get it off your chest." Was I about to hear the woman's confession? I didn't think murder was a justifiable act in general, but if she'd killed her husband because of his disloyalty, I could at least grasp it in principle, whether I condoned it or not.

"Perhaps you're right," she said. After taking a few deep breaths, she was clearly about to say something when her cell phone rang.

"Let it go to voicemail," I urged her. I couldn't afford to have her distracted at the moment.

She looked at her caller ID and said, "I'm sorry, but I've got to take this. Hello? No. No! Forget it! It's never going to happen!"

After she hung up, I asked, "Is everything okay?"

"Not by a long shot. I've got to take care of this right now. I've had all that I'm going to take."

"Who just called you, Lori?" I asked her.

The widow just shook her head and walked out, leaving most of her coffee and donut behind. I thought about running after her, or following her at the very least, but as I stood there trying to decide what to do, I realized that she'd talk when she was ready, and not a moment before.

"What was that all about?" Emma asked as she came back out front.

"You don't want to know," I said. "You know what? It's close enough to closing time not to matter. How are things in back?"

"I've got it all wrapped up," she said as she collected Lori's cup and plate. As Emma studied the display case, she said, "We've got seven donuts left. Do you have any plans for them?"

"No, they are yours if you want them," I said.

"I think I'll take them to Dad, if you don't mind. He had to go back to the presses for another printing of today's paper. It's been a huge event for him, and I want to help him celebrate."

"That's fine by me," I said as I locked the front door and started working on the day's report.

I was twenty dollars off, which was bad enough, but what made it worse was that I had more than I should have. How had I shortchanged my customers enough to collect that much more than I was supposed to?

I was still trying to figure it out when Emma walked out. "I'm finished in back." She frowned when she saw that I had the money laid out on the counter in stacks, after counting it three times and getting the same total. "Suzanne, you're going to kill me."

"Why would I do that?" I asked, distracted by my mistake.

"During your book club meeting, I found a twenty-dollar bill on the floor. I didn't know what to do with it, so I stuck it in the cash drawer without giving it another thought. I'm betting you are exactly twenty dollars off, right?"

"Right," I said, pulling one of the twenties from the stack and setting it aside. "That's good to know."

"It would have been even better earlier, right?"

"It's no problem, Emma," I said, relieved that I hadn't cheated anyone. If someone came in over the next few days and asked about their lost twenty, I'd be ready, and if they didn't, I'd put it in the tip jar and try to forget about it. "I'm ready if you are."

"Let's go, then," she said, grabbing the partial box of donuts and heading for the door.

I was surprised to find that Grace was outside waiting for me. "You could have always come inside and waited," I told her as Emma said her good-byes to both of us.

"I could have, but then you might have put me to work," she answered with a grin. "I've waded through enough paperwork to take some time off this afternoon. What's the plan?"

"I thought we might grab a bite to eat and then head back to Union Square. Should we eat at the Boxcar Grill or hit Napoli's again?"

Grace frowned. "That's a real dilemma. I want to be able to fit into my clothes, so maybe we should skip the Italian place. Then again, it's so delicious, I think I can be persuaded to forget about my waistline and eat there again if you try the least little bit."

I had to laugh. I could smell a donut and gain two pounds, while Grace had always had a metabolism that seemed to convert calories consumed into smiles.

Sometimes it drove me crazy, and I was glad I loved her so much, or I might have killed her.

"Let's throw caution to the wind," I said. "I'll brave a repeat visit to Napoli's if you will."

"What are we waiting for, then?" she asked. "There's no ice on the roads, and I need to drop something off in Union Square anyway, so let's take my company car."

"Are you sure?" I knew that Grace's employer wasn't thrilled when their people used company cars for personal transportation.

"Positive," she said. "Besides, you deserve to ride in style every now and then."

"I'm not about to argue with you," I said, happily sliding onto the passenger seat of her stylish vehicle.

As she drove to Union Square, I said, "I had a few unusual visitors at the donut shop today."

"Did Elvis and Nixon show up together?" she asked with a grin.

"No, but it wouldn't have surprised me much more than who did come by. Gwen was standing outside waiting for me when I opened." I told her what Greg's girlfriend had shared with me.

"So, she's really gone?" Grace asked me.

"I'm not sure. I called the chief as soon as I could, and I have a hunch he was going to track her down."

"You said that you had a few visitors. Who else came by?"

"Lori Whitmore," I said. "She admitted that she'd lied about knowing Gwen, but when I pressed her on the idea that her husband was writing bad loans, she flatly denied it."

"Much like she did when you asked her if Greg had a girlfriend yesterday?" Grace reminded me.

"She was adamant that Greg would never do anything illegal. It wasn't that he was so honest. He just hated the idea of going to jail. I believed her when she said it, but then again, I didn't think she knew about Gwen, either. Lori was about to tell me something else when she got a phone call and left the donut shop abruptly. I have no idea who was on the other end, but she was visibly shaken by the call."

"After we finish up in Union Square, we should track her down and ask her," Grace suggested. "Maybe we can get her to open up if we approach her together."

"Why not? It's at least worth a shot," I said.

Soon enough, Grace parked in front of Napoli's, and we headed for the front door. I could almost taste the ravioli when I felt my heart sink.

"*Closed for Lunch?* What's going on?" I asked Grace as we read the sign together.

"Hang on," she said. Studying the fine print below, she read aloud, "*Due to the overnight failure of our refrigeration system, we have been forced to close for lunch today in order to have it repaired and to resupply our larder. With any luck, we'll be up and running this evening, so try us again then. Sorry for the inconvenience.*"

"Oh, no. That's terrible," I said, sympathizing with Angelica and her daughters.

"Because we can't eat, or because they had to shut the place down?" Grace asked.

"We can still eat, just not here," I said. "I've had equipment problems before myself. What a nightmare. I wonder if there's anything we can do to help them."

"I have a feeling they have their hands full at the moment," Grace said. "Knowing Angelica, if we offer to help, she'll find a way to feed us, come what may, and she really can't afford to take the time away from getting up and running again."

"You're right. Let's see if we can find something else to eat in town."

"Good luck with that," Grace said. "Can you imagine anywhere that has *anything* near what the DeAngelis women offer?"

"I'd be happy with a flat soda and a stale sandwich at this point," I said.

"Be careful what you wish for," Grace said. "You just might get it."

We found a little diner near the bank that served breakfast and lunch, so we decided to give it a try. As we walked in, I was surprised to see Benny paying his tab at the register.

"What a coincidence. We were just coming to see you," I said with a smile.

"Sorry, but I can't talk. I'm late as it is."

He was gone so quickly that he almost forgot his change in his effort to get away from us.

"Was it just me, or was he not very happy to see us?" I asked Grace with a grin after he left.

"The man practically sprinted out of here the second we showed up," she agreed.

"Maybe we're making progress after all," I said. "If we've got our suspects on edge, we might just get lucky and one of them will do something stupid."

"One can only hope," Grace said as she grabbed a table for us both. We ordered and ate two nondescript meals. I knew after paying that Napoli's had nothing to worry about, at least not from that place.

When we got to the bank, we ignored the woman up front, smiling and waving at Benny as we approached his desk.

He didn't look all that happy to see us. "Listen, I have an important client coming in three minutes, and I have to get ready for the meeting."

I pulled out Momma's check and kept my fingers over the signature line so he couldn't see that it was unsigned. "More important than this?"

His eyes widened a little at the sight of all of those zeroes, but they quickly contracted again as he glanced behind us. Calvin

Trinket was making his way over to us, albeit a little slowly as an older woman stopped him by grabbing his arm and complaining about something. "Girls, is that legit?"

"Will you talk to us if it is?" I countered.

"That all depends. Do you want to open an account, or is it just to get me to talk more about Greg Whitmore?"

"What do you think, Benny? You're a smart man. You do the math."

"That's what I thought," he said. "I can't help you," he said regretfully, still looking at the check in my hand.

I put it away. "Very well. If you won't speak with us, then we'll just have to tell the police chief investigating Greg's murder that you refused to cooperate with us."

"Him again? He was here yesterday." Benny scowled. "If I talk to you, can you get him off my back?"

"We'll see what we can do. That's all we can promise," Grace said, "but if I were you, I'd take us up on our offer."

Benny thought about that for ten seconds before he sighed. "Fine. Just not here, and not now," he said. "Meet me at the diner where we ran into each other in half an hour. I'm going to claim to have a doctor's appointment, and I'll meet you there."

"Fine," I said as I felt someone's presence directly behind me.

"Ladies, I'm surprised to see you back again so soon. I trust you're feeling better today?" he asked me.

I'd nearly forgotten my feigned illness. "I'm just fine. One of the reasons we came by was to see Gwen. Why isn't she at her desk this morning?"

Trinket didn't even skip a beat. "She's had vacation time scheduled for months," he said smoothly. "No worries. She'll be back sometime late next week."

The slickness with which he lied amazed me. Gwen had promised me that she was going to be AWOL, and yet her boss acted as though her absence was completely expected. "What did you want to see her about, if I may ask?"

"She said she'd be able to direct us to the right person to handle this," I said as I held the check up again, still hiding the fact that it hadn't been signed. "My mother is having second thoughts about withdrawing her money from your bank."

"Why, that's wonderful news! I'd be glad to handle that for you personally," he said as he tried to hustle the two of us out of Benny's office.

"I was just about to help them myself, sir," Benny said. Was there some reason he didn't want us talking to his boss, or was he just trying to tweak the man?

"You already have an appointment though, or am I wrong?"

"No, you're right," he agreed.

"Then as I said, I'll take care of these fine ladies." The dismissal was clear. I liked this man even less than I had the day before, if that were even possible.

We followed the branch manager back to his office, where he tried to close the door.

"Let's leave that open, shall we?" I suggested.

"As you wish. Now, let's see that check. I'll have it processed and you'll be on your way in no time."

"First, I'd like to know a few things about your bank. We've recently learned that you've been accused of making some bad loans. Is there any truth to those rumors?"

The man's face turned white at the question, and I knew that Gwen must have been at least a little right about it. "I don't know what you're talking about," he said, doing his best to bluster his way out of it. "I can personally assure you that nothing of that nature is going on here. We have a solid reputation for honesty and trustworthiness that cannot be disputed."

"So, you're saying that if something bad *was* going on, you don't know about it?" Grace asked. It was a trick question, designed to make him admit that he was either a dupe or a liar.

"I'm saying that I refuse to acknowledge your basic premise," he answered, not really answering her at all.

"Where were you the night of the murder, Mr. Trinket?" I asked him point-blank.

He looked startled by the direct question. "Do you honestly think I had anything to do with what happened to Greg Whitmore?"

"We'll be able to answer that question better once we hear your answer," I said.

"I was here working late, not that it is anyone else's business. Now, about that check…"

As he reached for it, I tucked it back into my pocket. "I'm afraid I'll be holding onto it for a little while longer."

He bit his lower lip for a moment before answering. "Then evidently our business here is done." As he stood, he said, "If you should change your mind at any future date, please know that we are here to serve you." It was as complete a brushoff as I'd ever received in my life.

Grace and I allowed him to lead us out of the bank, and once we were outside, I said, "Let's get over to that diner and wait for Benny."

"We could just wait for him here in the parking lot," she suggested.

"Do you think there's any chance at all he'll talk to us with his boss so close by?"

"No, you're right. Let's go."

We did just that, ordering two cups of dismal coffee and a single slice of pie to split that wasn't much better, and we waited.

And waited.

And waited.

After an hour and a half, I turned to Grace. "He's not showing up, is he?"

"It doesn't look like it," she said.

"What can I say? You were right and I was wrong," I said.

"As much as I'd like to revel in that declaration, your point was valid at the time. It wouldn't have done us any good to wait for him in the parking lot."

"So, what do we do now?" I asked.

"Let's go see if he's still at the bank. I wonder why he changed his mind."

"I don't know, but I don't appreciate being jerked around like this, do you?"

"No, ma'am."

He wasn't at his desk, either. When I asked the receptionist where he was, she told us that he had suddenly taken ill the moment we'd left, and he said that he wouldn't be back that day. Had he decided to meet us and then changed his mind at the last second, or was there a chance that he was actually ill? Either way, it appeared that we weren't going to get Benny's story that day either way. I kept waiting for Calvin Trinket to see us, but he was nowhere to be found, either. What was going on here?

The next question was what to do next.

We walked back to Grace's car, but I put a hand on hers, stopping her before we reached it. "What is it?" she asked me.

Instead of answering aloud, I pointed to a spot in the alley behind the bank, where Calvin Trinket was having an earnest conversation with what appeared to be two very angry men.

CHAPTER 17

"**S**HOULD WE CALL FOR HELP?" Grace asked me softly as we watched one of the men continually jab Trinket in the chest with his meaty index finger.

"Who do you suggest we call?" I asked.

"I was thinking along the lines of the police."

"What would we tell them, that two men are being mean to the bank manager?" I asked as I continued to watch in fascination. The usually smooth branch manager was clearly terrified of the two men who were accosting him, and the scary part was that nobody was screaming. I've often found softly voiced threats worse than shouting.

Trinket kept trying to back up to get away from the jabs, but the men kept matching him step for step.

Grace tugged at my arm. "Suzanne, we need to do something, or this is going to end badly."

"I've got an idea," I said as I started walking toward the confrontation. "Follow my lead."

"I always do," she said with grim determination.

"Mr. Trinket, there you are," I said loudly, catching the three men equally off guard. "My husband's going to be a little late. He had a meeting with the other state police inspectors who are in town, and a few of them are tagging along. I hope that's all right."

I had to give the man credit; it didn't take him long to catch on. "That will be fine. Sorry, I got held up here, but we can go ahead and get started." He looked tentatively at the two men, and the smaller of the two nodded after a second of deliberation. "Will you gentlemen excuse me?"

"Fine. Go to your meeting. We'll talk again soon," one of the men said. To emphasize his point, he jabbed Trinket one last time as he added, "It's going to be very soon, so don't go anywhere."

"I wouldn't dream of it," Trinket said as he hurried toward us.

"Thank you both," he said softly as he walked past us. "We need to get inside, and I mean right now."

Grace and I followed him into the bank, past the receptionist, and into his office, where he promptly shut the door behind us. The branch manager seemed to collapse inward the moment he was back in his inner sanctum.

"Since we just saved your worthless hide, do you mind telling us what that was all about?" Grace asked. I glanced at her, surprised by the tone she'd taken but trusting that she knew what she was doing.

"What?" Trinket asked her incredulously, as though he were just coming out of some kind of trance. "What did you just say to me?"

"That's it," Grace said as she turned to me. "I'm calling the police chief. If Mr. Trinket here won't speak with us, he'll just have to talk to the cops."

Calvin Trinket nodded absently, as though he were lost in another world. After a few moments, he nodded with a certain fatality. "Yes. That's a good idea. Call them."

I had a feeling that Grace had been bluffing.

Well, he'd just called her bluff.

"What should I tell them?" Grace asked as she pulled out her cell phone. What else could she do? The only option she had now was to play out her hand.

"Tell him that I'm ready to talk," the manager said as he slumped down in his leather chair.

"Okay, I'm here," Chief Grant said after we met him outside the bank manager's office forty-five minutes later. There was a spirit of cooperation between police chiefs in our area, and I knew they frequently worked in each other's jurisdictions. "Has he said anything to you two yet?"

"Not a word," I admitted.

"But he's ready to confess to killing Greg Whitmore, right?"

"We're not entirely sure of that," Grace replied, hedging her bets a little. "All he said was that we should call you and that he was ready to talk. We don't have a clue what he's about to tell you." In a lower voice, she asked, "Is there any way we can go in there with you? We won't say a word, but we brought this to you. It's only fair."

"I don't know about fair, but it's okay with me if he doesn't raise any objections. I have to ask him, though."

"That's fine," I said before Grace could argue with him. It was the best chance we had of getting into that office, and I didn't want to risk blowing it.

"I understand you want to speak with me," Chief Grant said as we all walked into the bank manager's office together.

"Yes, it's long past time for this particular conversation. I'm finally willing to admit that things went farther than they ever should have."

The police chief held up a hand. "Before you say anything, I need to stop you."

"Are you reading me my rights?" he asked dully.

"I can't very well do that, since I don't know what you're about to tell me. I need to know if you have any problem whatsoever with letting Suzanne and Grace stay for this."

Trinket didn't even hesitate. "I don't care. Everybody's going to know what happened soon enough."

The chief turned to us and nodded but put a finger to his

lips, warning us. The message was clear: we were to be seen and not heard, no matter what.

"Now, go on," Chief Grant said.

The bank manager nodded, and then he spoke in a voice that was nearly a whisper, as though he could lessen what he was about to tell us in some way. "It started out innocently enough. One of our customers was going to be late on a loan several months back, and he came to me for an extension. He'd been late before, and I told him that this time he had to pay promptly, or there would be consequences. An hour later, a man I'd never met before visited me in my office."

"What was his name?" the chief asked.

"I'd rather not say just yet," Trinket replied.

"Fine. Go on." Good for the chief. I knew he would get the main part of the story first, and any details he needed would come after. I had a hunch that once Calvin Trinket opened up, there would be no stopping the floodgate of information.

"Let's call this man Joseph for now," Trinket said. "He asked me if I knew who he was, and I admitted that I did not. He seemed pleased by that response, and then he went on to explain that he had dealings with a great many people on both sides of the law and that he was a good friend to have but an even worse enemy. Joseph told me that he'd consider it a personal favor if I'd extend the loan, and to be honest with you, there was something scary about the man. Not the way he looked, you understand, but his calm outward appearance. I got the message that a yes would be well received, but a no would bring swift retribution. What can I say? I caved in and granted the extension. That was my first mistake. Once he knew I could be intimidated, he started asking for more and more favors, and I just found it easier to go along with him, especially since he was recommending new clients to me right and left, and our deposits were soaring."

"How much of that was tainted money?" the chief asked

somberly. It was the exact same question I would have asked myself, and I was dying to hear the answer.

"I couldn't prove that any of it was at the time," Trinket said in his own defense, and then he seemed to shrink into himself a little. "I had a hunch, though. The deposits were all under the reporting limit of ten thousand dollars, but not by a lot. On paper, it was a good deal."

"But then the other shoe dropped," the chief said, nudging him a little.

"He started demanding that we issue loans to folks with no or terrible credit, offering me his unofficial and personal guarantee that they would be paid back in full."

"So, you became a money launderer for the mob," the chief said. "Is that why you killed Greg Whitmore? Did he find out what you were up to?"

"I didn't kill Greg!" Trinket protested. "Sure, I made some bad mistakes, but I didn't commit murder."

"Why were you two fighting so much, then?" I asked, forgetting my promise to remain silent for the moment.

"He figured out what I was up to," Trinket said, "and Greg was furious. He discovered that I'd issued some of those loans in his name without his knowledge, and he wasn't about to go to jail for me. He gave me one week to come clean, or he was going to go straight to the police with what he knew."

"I don't know, Mr. Trinket," Chief Grant said softly. "It seems to me as though you just gave yourself a powerful motive for murder, either for you or your friend Joseph."

"I can assure you, he didn't do it or have it done for him," Trinket said quickly and then turned to us. "Did you two tell him how you saved me this afternoon?"

"No," I said.

"Talk, Suzanne," the chief said.

"Two thugs were threatening him in the alley, and we managed to extract him from the situation before things could escalate."

"For the moment, at least," Trinket said. "They had a message for me from Joseph. They said that when I killed Greg Whitmore, I'd signed my own death warrant. They couldn't have done it; they were blaming me for his murder! The message was that it had been the stupidest thing I could have done, since it was going to bring scrutiny down on all of us. No matter how much I protested that I hadn't touched Greg, they wouldn't believe me! There's no way Joseph had anything to do with it. He didn't even know everything I'd done with the loans until after Greg was already dead!"

That made sense in its own way. Besides, I was fairly sure the men in question wouldn't go to the trouble of dragging Greg's dead body on a sled through town in the middle of an ice storm, especially taking the time to change him into a Santa suit first.

"I can see that, but how can I know that you didn't do it yourself?" the chief asked him, evidently taking the thug's innocence to heart, at least with this particular homicide.

"I was here all night!" Calvin said. "I was trying to put something together to shift the blame away from me."

"And onto Greg?" I asked.

"That's not important," he said, which was a clear yes in my mind.

"How can I know that's true?" the chief asked.

"Check the security tapes. I was in my office from six p.m. until five the next morning. I *couldn't* have killed Greg Whitmore."

"We'll look into it," he said. "In the meantime, you've got some other actions you need to answer for."

"Call whoever you want. I'll talk to the FBI, the FDIC, the federal bank examiners, the IRS, anybody. You have to protect me, though. If Joseph finds out that I talked to you, I'll be dead by nightfall."

"Don't worry. You'll be safe enough with me," Chief Grant said. "Why don't we continue this conversation back in my office? We can make all of the calls we need to along the way."

"Do I have to ride in the back of your squad car?" Trinket asked Chief Grant pitifully.

"Right now, that should be the least of your worries," the chief said.

"At least do me one favor. Don't handcuff me and walk me out of my own bank as though I were some kind of criminal."

"Fine," the chief said reluctantly. It was funny in a sad kind of way. This man had just admitted to the three of us that he was felonious on several different levels, and yet he didn't want to be treated like a lawbreaker. Just because he hadn't shot Greg Whitmore didn't mean that he was a good guy by any definition of the term.

"Thank you for the call," the chief said to us as he escorted Trinket out of the building, sans handcuffs.

"We were happy to help," I said.

"Will I see you later?" Grace asked him.

"It really depends on how long it takes to clear up this mess," he said with a smile.

"I'll wait up, no matter how long it takes," she answered gently.

"Then you've got yourself a deal."

"Well, at least we can take Calvin Trinket's name off our suspect list," I said as Grace and I watched the men drive away in the chief's squad car.

"That still leaves us Benny, Gwen, and Lori," she said, "and we can't find two out of three of them. Any ideas on what we should do next?"

"I say we go talk to Lori again. After all, she shouldn't be that hard to find," I suggested as we got into Grace's car and headed back to April Springs. "She was about to tell me something important. I just know it."

"Then we need to press her a little harder and see if she cracks. It's going to be unsatisfying somehow if the bitter estranged wife did it," Grace said.

"How so?"

"If Lori was the one who pulled the trigger, it's going to seem more like a case for the police than a pair of amateur sleuths."

"You know what? I'm fine with that," I said as we headed back to town. "I just want to see whoever did it caught and punished for their crime. If Chief Grant solves it and makes the arrest without any help from us, it won't hurt me one little bit. We're doing our part, and that's really all that we can do."

"You're right. Sorry, I lost track of why we were doing this for one split second. Let's go talk to Lori," she said.

CHAPTER 18

"Hi, Penny," I said as my friend opened her front door.

"She's not here, Suzanne, and even if she were, I'm not sure she'd be all that excited about talking to you or Grace. The last time we spoke, she seemed pretty upset."

"We're just trying to help," Grace said. "Can we come in?"

"For a minute or two," she said as she stepped aside. "What's the matter, don't you trust me? Feel free to search the place."

It was clear that Penny wasn't that pleased to see us, either.

"Come on. Don't be that way. You can see that we're just trying to find out what happened to Greg, can't you?"

"The truth of the matter is that I'm trying my best not to get involved. After all, you're all my friends." She frowned for a moment before she added, "Lori's got a point, though. She's torn up about Greg's murder, and it doesn't help that they were estranged when it happened. Piled on top of that is the fact that most of the people in town are sure that she's the one who did it, including the chief of police, evidently, and it adds up to a full plate that nobody wants on their table."

"You're right, of course," I said. "I'm sorry if we've made it harder on her than it was already."

"I know that your hearts are in the right places," Penny conceded. "I just hate seeing Lori going through so much, and there's nothing I can do about it."

"Come on, you're doing a lot. You're putting her up, aren't you? Without you, she wouldn't even have a place to live."

Penny shrugged. "It doesn't feel like I'm doing that much to me." She glanced at her watch again as she said, "I hate to be rude, but I have to get to the hospital. We've had a few nurses suddenly quit, and I'm pulling more shifts than I'm happy about. It will be nice when payday rolls around, but right now I'm not exactly loving it."

We walked out with her, but before she could drive away, Grace asked her, "Penny, you don't have an old-fashioned sled lying around by any chance, do you?"

"Grace, it's been ages since I've sledded down a hill. When was the last time we even had enough snow to matter? And why the sudden interest in my winter activities?"

"Who else has asked you lately?" I asked her.

"The chief of police. I'll tell you what I told him. I used to live on one when I was a kid, but I haven't ridden it in ages. It made the move with me though, and I had the guys stick it in the garage, along with all of the junk the previous owner left behind. The last I saw of it, it was hanging from the rafters out there," she said as she pointed behind the house.

"Would you mind if we took a peek while we're here?" Grace asked.

"Feel free. It's not locked. Somebody broke into it last week, not that it took a master thief to do it. I haven't been able to park my car in there since I got the place, and based on how much junk is out there, I never will. Save yourself the trouble, though. Chief Grant already looked, and he came up empty."

"We might poke around anyway, if you're sure you don't mind."

"Like I said, suit yourself." She paused to grin at us. "Speaking of which, keep in mind that we give tetanus shots at the hospital seven days a week."

"Is it really that bad?" I asked her, smiling back.

"It's not good. I'll see you both later," she said.

"Is it even worth checking out, since Stephen couldn't find anything?" Grace asked me after Penny was gone.

"Why not? We're here," I said as I started walking around the back of the house to where the old garage stood. It looked as though the only thing keeping it erect was a string of termites holding hands, and I could see that Penny had only been halfway joking about the danger of going inside, but I still had to see for myself.

"We don't even have a flashlight," Grace reminded me as I examined the busted lock. The truth of the matter was that the lock was just fine; the hasp it was attached to had been ripped off the side of the garage, though. I looked at the wood where it had been attached. There were fresh claw marks on it, as though an angry bear had broken in.

"Someone pried it loose," I said, taking a photo of it with my phone before I forgot.

"Why would anyone bother breaking in here?" Grace asked as we pulled the big doors open. A swarm of dust mites seemed to greet our arrival, and I could see several large spider webs in the limited sunshine coming in. Beyond the opening, the entire garage was steeped in shadows, and I knew that it was going to be tough to find anything inside without a strong light. I didn't happen to have one of those police flashlight monstrosities with me, but I did have something on my phone I could use. I turned on the application and moved the bright, though limited, light across the space. It was filled nearly to the rafters with old newspapers, long-abandoned mason jars, discarded Christmas ornaments that hadn't made the cut this year, watering cans with more holes than any vessel should ever have, yards and yards of rotting canvas, and a host of things I didn't even recognize.

"Stephen searched the entire place?" Grace asked me in bewilderment. "Did he bring an entire crew with him?"

"Come on. It's not that bad," I said as I waved away a few cobwebs that drifted near my face. I wasn't a big fan of spiders, but at least this one was long gone.

Or so I hoped.

I was about to peel back some of the old canvas when Grace screamed!

"What is it?" I asked as I turned back toward her with my light.

"Something just landed in my hair," she said, absolutely horrified.

I saw it instantly and reached out and pulled a strand of dry grass from her hair. "It's okay. It's just hay. See?"

She looked at it skeptically. "Are you sure that's all it was?"

I did another search, this one coming up empty. "One hundred percent. You're good to go."

"Sorry. Sometimes my imagination gets the better of me."

"No need to apologize," I told her. "If this had been Halloween instead of Christmas, I would have reacted exactly the same."

"No," she corrected me, "if it had happened to you instead of me, you would have screamed even louder than I just did."

"I'm not sure that's entirely possible," I said with a grin.

"Maybe not," she answered good-naturedly. "Regardless, I believe I'm finished with this particular task. Feel free to keep searching all you like by yourself, though. I'll be waiting at the car."

"No worries," I said as I went back to the canvas and flipped it open. Before she could go, I said, "Grace, come here."

"What is it, Suzanne? I'm sorry, but I don't think I can help you."

"All I'm saying is that you're going to want to see this," I said.

"What did you find, another body?" she asked lightly, trying to break the tension in the air.

It didn't work. "No, but I believe I just found what was used to move Greg Whitmore."

I pulled the canvas away and showed her my find. There was something fresh staining the wood of the old sled, and the runners had a glistening layer of rust on them, as if they'd been exposed to the weather recently.

We'd found the sled everyone had been looking for, in the worst place possible for Lori Whitmore.

And that's when I heard a voice behind me ask, "What exactly do you two think you're doing in here? I'm calling the police."

And a split second later, another voice behind her said, "There's no need for that, since I'm already here."

CHAPTER 19

"L ET'S EVERYONE JUST TAKE IT real easy," Chief Grant said as I turned to see him holding his gun on Lori. "Nobody needs to do anything crazy here."

Lori noticed his gun immediately. "What are you doing? I found these two breaking into Penny's shed and you're holding a gun on *me*?"

"We weren't breaking in," I explained. "Penny gave us her permission to search the place. You can call her at the hospital to confirm that if you'd like."

"What in the world is that doing there?" the chief asked as he stared at the sled I'd just uncovered.

"It could have been easy to miss," I said, giving him the benefit of the doubt. In fact, it had been so easy to find that I wondered how he could have possibly missed it if he'd even bothered to search the garage at all, but I wasn't about to point that out to him, whether he was holding a gun at the moment or not.

"I looked there, and it wasn't in the garage yesterday," he said definitively.

"Well, it's here now," Grace said.

"I certainly didn't put it there," Lori said defiantly.

"Why don't we talk about that in a second?" the chief asked. "How about if everyone steps outside? I'd like to see your hands up in the air."

"*All* of us?" Grace asked.

"If you don't mind."

I put mine up quickly, and Grace, though unhappy about the situation, did so as well. That left Lori, who was stubbornly refusing to cooperate.

Chief Grant wasn't having any of that, though. "I'm telling you one last time. If you don't do as I say, I'm going to treat you as hostile and assume you are armed."

It was amazing how quickly the woman's hands shot into the air. "I'm not armed! I wasn't going to hurt them. I was just shocked to find someone in Penny's garage. This is all just one big misunderstanding."

"Then why were you sneaking up on us?" Grace asked her.

"What was I going to do, lock you in? The hasp is broken, remember? I was just trying to see what you were up to. I wasn't going to do anything."

Once the chief saw that we were all unarmed, he did a quick but thorough examination of Lori and then me. Reluctantly, he turned to Grace. "Sorry about this."

"Go on. I might enjoy it, or I would under different circumstances."

Though he didn't lay a hand on any of us, it was clear that we weren't sporting any weapons. Once the police chief was satisfied that none of us were armed, he relaxed and put his own weapon away. "Lori, I'd like it if you'd come down to my office so we could discuss a few things."

"I'm through talking to you! Are you arresting me?" she asked, clearly made indignant by the turn of events.

"That depends. Are you refusing to have another friendly little chat with me?" he asked her politely. She might have mistaken it for such at any rate, but I knew better. It was a challenge, and if I were in Lori's shoes, I'd do what the man was asking voluntarily before it became mandatory instead.

The widow must have caught a bit of it as well. "We can talk, but I'm telling you, I've never seen that sled before, and I didn't kill my husband."

"Then this should be a breeze," Chief Grant said as he held the back open for her.

"Honestly? Must I ride in the back like some kind of common criminal?"

"You have to sign a waiver to ride up front with me," he explained.

"Fine. I'll sign it," she insisted.

Chief Grant just shrugged. "Sorry, but I'm fresh out. No worries. It's not a very long ride." After Lori was in the back of the squad car, the chief put on gloves and collected the sled, stowing it in the back of the squad car before turning to us. "Sorry about that earlier, but I didn't have much choice, given the circumstances."

"No worries," I said to him quickly.

"Well, maybe a few worries," Grace added as she arched one eyebrow. "Stephen, is she really stupid enough to use that sled to move Greg's body and then return it to the garage after you searched it?"

He appeared to be pleased that she'd softened her tone with him. "Grace, the amount of stupidity displayed by the common criminal would blow your mind."

"What are you going to do with her?" I asked him.

The chief of police did his best to grin, but there wasn't an ounce of warmth in it. "Just like I said. We're going to have ourselves a little chat and see what develops from there."

Once they were gone, Grace looked at me and asked, "What do you think?"

"I don't know at this point. It's entirely possible that Lori did it, but I'm not sure that I'm finished with Benny and Gwen yet."

"Then I suggest we find them and move forward," Grace said.

Only it turned out that there was no need for us to do anything else when one of them found us before we could leave Penny's in search of our last two suspects. We'd stepped back inside to have one last look around when we heard someone else approaching.

"I just saw the police chief driving away with Lori in the backseat," Benny said breathlessly as he joined us in the garage. "He told me you both were back here. Did Lori really kill Greg? I don't believe it."

"We're not sure, either," I told him. "Why are you here, Benny? You stood us up today!"

"I had to. I've been out looking for Gwen since we spoke last," he said, looking behind his shoulder as he answered.

"I'm sure that she's long gone," I told him.

"That's what you think. She's after me. The woman has gone completely psycho! She killed Greg, and now she's after me!"

CHAPTER 20

"**W**HAT MAKES YOU SAY THAT?" I asked him. His paranoia was catching. I wasn't sure how safe we were standing there in that garage, where it was easy for someone, especially someone crazy, to sneak up on us.

"I didn't want to say anything at the bank today, but she came to my house last night," he said. "She kept ranting and raving about how I killed Greg! I kept assuring her that I didn't do it, but she wouldn't believe me. She said that I might be able to fool the police but that she knew! The woman was insane! I managed to slam the door in her face, but she yelled that she'd be back, and the next time she'd have a gun. I decided that I needed to find her and convince her that I was innocent before she could do something stupid."

"Why would you look for her here, though?" Grace asked him reasonably.

It was a fair question, and I backed a little farther into the garage, since Benny had completely cut off our escape. Was he telling us the truth about Gwen, or was he spinning his own web to entrap us?

"She actually thinks I did it with Lori's help," he said. "I realized I'd better watch Penny's place in case Gwen tried to hurt Lori."

"Why didn't you join us when we were all back here before?"

I asked, moving closer to one of the piles of clutter, hoping that there was some kind of weapon there if I needed it.

"I had to go to the bathroom, and the closest one was at the gas station on the corner. I got back just as the chief was driving away."

"There you are!" a woman's voice shouted angrily behind Benny.

Gwen West was standing in the sunlight, and I had to admit that Benny had probably been right in his estimation of Gwen's state of mind. She looked as though she were possessed by demons as she pointed a gun at all of us. "You aren't nearly as smart as you think you are, Benny. You might have gotten away with killing Greg, but you're not going to kill me!"

"I told you she was crazy," Benny protested. "I didn't do it, Gwen. Now put that gun down, and we'll get you some help."

"The only help I need is for someone to call the police," she said. Keeping the gun pointed at Benny, she said, "Suzanne, call the authorities." When I failed to do so immediately, the gun came back toward me. "I said call them!"

I reached for my phone, wondering how this was all going to play out. I started to do as I was told, and I'd just begun to dial the police chief's number when Benny made a quick step toward me, knocking the phone out of my hand.

Gwen yelled out, "Get away from her!"

The gun was pointing at both of us now.

"Shoot me and she dies, too," Benny said harshly, and I felt the prick of a knife at my neck. It appeared that Gwen wasn't nearly as crazy as she had once seemed.

CHAPTER 21

"**D**rop it!" Benny shouted at Gwen, who looked torn by the command.

"Shoot him!" I shouted at her. I had a better chance of surviving that way, and I knew it. We all did. If Greg got the upper hand, there wasn't much doubt that none of us would leave that garage alive.

"I can't! My aim isn't that good," she wailed, and I could see that she was at the breaking point. One slight push and she'd tumble over the edge from reason to insanity.

"I don't care!" I said loudly.

"Do you *want* to die, Suzanne?" Benny asked, the knife blade pricking my skin again.

"No, but if I'm going to go, I want it to be on my terms."

"I'm sorry. I just can't do it," Gwen said as she collapsed to the ground, the gun bouncing harmlessly off the floor of the garage.

"Very good," Benny said. He sounded pleased with himself.

I was going to do my best not to let him feel that way for much longer.

I didn't have a weapon, but I had something that might sound like one.

He ordered Grace, "Pick up the gun and bring it to me slowly. Grab it by the barrel. If your hand touches the grip, your best friend is going to die."

Grace looked at me with fear in her eyes, but I did my best

to reassure her. I squinted to give her a sign to follow my lead and hoped she'd be able to figure it out.

The timing on this would be critical.

As she leaned over to pick the gun up, it was time to make my move.

I'd seen some discarded glass ornaments on the floor of the garage just behind me, so as carefully as I could manage it, I stomped on the one closest to me.

It sounded as though someone had fired a shot directly behind us.

Benny, startled by the sound, dropped his guard for a split second and took the knife from my throat as he whirled around to face the unknown danger lurking behind us.

Grace was quicker than I ever imagined she could be. She grabbed the gun, by the handle and not the barrel, and by the time Benny realized what was happening, she had it pointed at his heart.

"You don't have the guts to pull the trigger," he said as he started for me with the knife.

Grace fired a shot into the rafters, deafening us all for a few moments. The smell of spent gunpowder filled the air, and I saw Benny's knife hit the floor.

All Gwen could do was whimper even louder than she had been doing before.

"Suzanne, call Stephen," Grace ordered, and I was glad to oblige.

After I made the call and we had Stephen cornered, I asked, "Why did you kill him, Benny?"

"Does it matter at this point?" he asked sullenly.

"It does to us," I said.

"The fool came to me and told me that he was going to expose Trinket! Did he honestly think Calvin was the *only* one working for the bad guys? I'd been doing the same thing myself. How do you think they recruited him? If Calvin went down, I knew I'd be going down with him."

"But why kill Greg? Weren't you worried it would lead to an investigation of all of you anyway?"

"I was going to take care of that," Benny said as he took a slow step backward. Did he think he was going to be able to escape us out the back through that mess? "All I needed was a little time," he whined, as though he were a boy with stolen toys. "I came to Greg's place to argue that he should delay reporting Calvin to the authorities, but he wouldn't listen to me. He wasn't about to go to jail. His dad served time when Greg was a boy; did you all know that? The image of visiting him in jail made him horrified of ever being accused of doing anything illegal. I spent ten minutes trying to change his mind, but when I couldn't, I knew what I had to do. He didn't leave me any choice."

"So you shot him," Grace said. "I'm surprised you came here with a knife if you had a gun all along."

I got it then. "You weren't here looking for Gwen, were you?" I asked. "I'm willing to bet that gun is somewhere near where we found the sled. You must have planted them just before we arrived. Grace, be careful."

"No worries, Suzanne. If he moves, he dies," she said, pointing the gun straight at his chest.

"You think you're so smart, don't you?" Benny asked, clearly deflated by us figuring out what he was up to.

"What I don't get is why the Santa suit, and why risk putting him in the park?" I asked him.

"I don't guess it matters anymore," Benny said. Once I'd figured out his desire to retrieve the murder weapon, the fight seemed to have gone straight out of him. "My fingerprints were all over that house, and I wanted to divert suspicion away from it. I found the suit in the back of his closet. Do you know how hard it is to change a dead man's clothes?" He shuddered a little from the memory of it. "Anyway, once I got him changed, I knew I couldn't just carry him through town over my shoulders. Greg had told me where Lori was staying, so I decided to snoop a little and see if there was anything over here I could use that might point suspicion toward her and not me. I broke into the shed, found the sled, and tied Greg to it. I figured nobody was out in the storm, but if they were, they'd think it was just a pair of crazy kids playing in the park."

"Why didn't you put the sled back where you found it after you were through?" I asked.

"I was going to, but then the storm started getting worse! I shoved the sled into my trunk and got out before I was trapped here! I meant to bring it back, but I didn't have a chance until a few minutes before the two of you showed up. I ditched the gun behind it, and if no one found it soon, I was going to call in a tip to the police or the newspaper that I'd seen a woman with it the night of the storm."

"So, you were going to frame Lori for the murder and Calvin and Greg for your crimes at the bank," I said. "You're quite the prize, aren't you?"

"Hey, if I don't look out for myself, who will?" he asked, trying and failing to justify his behavior, whether to us or himself I couldn't say.

"I'll take that," Chief Grant said softly as he walked up behind Grace and reached for the weapon still in her hand. "It's okay. You did good."

"I had to fire it once, so I did everything exactly how you taught me."

"Did you have to kill her?" he asked as he pointed to Gwen's body.

"No! I shot into the roof," Grace said. "Apart from a mental breakdown, she's fine."

Gwen finally pulled herself together, stood up, and then dusted herself off. "I didn't have a breakdown."

No matter how wrong she was, I wasn't going to argue with her. "How are you feeling now?"

"Better, now that the police are here," she said, her voice still a little shaky. "That was too close for comfort."

"We had it all under control," I assured her.

"That's what you think," Gwen replied. "There was only one bullet in that gun, and Grace wasted it shooting the roof of the garage."

After Chief Grant led Benny away in handcuffs, I turned to the women still there with me. "Gwen, I'm sorry I ever doubted you, even for an instant."

"It's okay," she said. "Benny may be a cold-blooded killer, but he's also smooth enough to be able to sell heat lamps in the desert." She looked around and then said sadly, "I need to get out of here."

"The garage? I agree," I said as we all walked outside.

"No, I'm talking about April Springs, Union Square, Maple Hollow, all of it. I need a fresh start, and now that I know what really happened to Greg, I'm going to find it, no matter how hard I have to search. I'll see you two at the station."

Chief Grant had asked us all to stop by for our statements, so the three of us made our way there. I couldn't blame Gwen. She'd undergone one traumatic experience after another, and sometimes a change of scenery was the only thing that could help. I just hoped that she remembered the most important part of it: wherever she went, she'd be taking herself with her. She'd have to change inside, just as she was shifting her surroundings to someplace new.

CHAPTER 22

W HEN I GOT HOME, I was shocked to find my Jeep parked in the driveway and Jake at the door. After nearly hugging the breath out of him, I asked my husband, "How did you get back home so soon?"

"The party was breaking up about the time the snowplows dug us out," he said. "I heard you've been busy."

"Who have you been talking to?" I asked him.

"I stopped by your mother's when I saw you weren't home," he explained. "Phillip told me all about Greg Whitmore."

"He couldn't have," I said.

"Why not?" Jake asked.

"Because I just found out the ending myself. Come on, let me make us something to eat, and I can tell you all about it."

"That sounds great to me. I'm starving," he said with a grin. "Oh, before I forget, your mother has lined up a contractor to start on the donut shop next week. She apologizes, but given the circumstances, it was the best she could do. No worries, she got three quotes, too. He's not one of her regular people, but the ice storm created a lot of havoc around town, and they're all going to be busy."

"It's so wonderful that I don't have to think about that," I said when I noticed he was grinning at me. "Why the smile?"

"Can't I just be happy that I'm back home where I belong?" he asked me.

"Yes, but something else is going on," I said.

"You know me too well. Do you happen to know how they harvest mistletoe in the mountains?"

"No," I said. "Do you know the population of Anchorage, Alaska?"

He looked puzzled. "What does that have to do with anything?"

"Nothing. I just thought we were asking each other random questions," I said happily, glad that he'd made it back safely to me, and sooner than expected, too.

"The reason I asked you about mistletoe is that I witnessed it firsthand. They use shotguns and shoot it out of the trees, if you can imagine that." Then he reached into his pocket and pulled out a sprig, holding it over my head and grinning again. "This one's never been used. Care to break it in with me?"

It was the one decoration our cottage was missing. I laughed as I threw myself into my husband's arms. The mistletoe went flying, but I didn't care. I didn't need an excuse to kiss my own husband.

After we finished our proper greeting, Jake hung the mistletoe over the doorway, and then he lit a fire as I rustled us up some food. With Christmas carols playing in the background, the tree's lights blinking on and off, and the fire crackling happily in the hearth, it couldn't have been more perfect if I'd planned it myself.

I didn't even mind not having snow outside.

For now, I was happy not to have any precipitation falling from the sky in any shape or form.

RECIPES

A Nice First Donut

If you've never tried to make donuts yourself, this is a good place to start. These are the first donuts I ever learned to make, and the recipe is one I revisit from time to time. There's something to be said for some of the more exotic donuts I make, but when a tried-and-true recipe is called for, you can't go wrong with this one.

Ingredients

- 4 1/2 cups bread flour (unbleached flour will do as well in a pinch)
- 1 cup granulated sugar
- 1 teaspoon baking soda
- 1/2 teaspoon cinnamon
- 1/2 teaspoon nutmeg
- 2 dashes of salt
- 1 egg, beaten
- 1/2 cup sour cream
- 1 cup buttermilk (whole or 2% milk can be substituted)
- 1½ to 2 quarts canola oil for frying (depending on the depth of your pot)

Directions

On the stovetop or in your donut fryer, add the canola oil and heat to 375 degrees F.

In a large mixing bowl, combine the flour, sugar, baking soda, cinnamon, nutmeg, and salt and sift into another bowl. Add the beaten egg to the dry mix, then add the sour cream and the liquid (milk or buttermilk) to the mixture and stir it all together lightly. You may need more liquid or flour to get the dough to a workable mix. This varies based on temperature and humidity. The dough shouldn't stick to your hands when you touch it, but it should be moist enough to remain flexible. Knead this mix lightly, then roll it out to about 1/4 of an inch. Take your donut hole cutter and press out your donut shapes, reserving the holes for a later frying. The cutters are inexpensive and worth having on hand, but if you don't have one readily available, two small glasses of varying diameters will do nicely as well.

Place 4 to 6 donuts in the oil at a time, being careful not to crowd them, and then let the donuts cook for two minutes on each side, flipping them halfway with a wooden skewer.

Once the donuts are golden brown, remove them to a cooling rack and sprinkle with powdered sugar or cinnamon or eat them plain.

Makes approximately 1 dozen donuts.

Apple Cider Donuts

We like these donuts in the fall when it's cider season, but you can make them any time of year for the fresh taste of autumn in a tasty little treat!

Ingredients

- 1 egg, beaten
- 2/3 cup brown sugar (light or dark works fine), packed tight
- 3 tablespoons unsalted butter, melted
- 1/2 cup apple cider (apple juice can be used in a pinch)
- 2 1/2 cups all-purpose flour
- 1/2 teaspoon cinnamon
- 1/2 teaspoon nutmeg
- 1 teaspoon baking powder
- 1/2 teaspoon baking soda
- 2 dashes salt
- 1½ to 2 quarts canola oil for frying (depending on the depth of your pot)

Directions

Heat enough canola oil to allow the donuts to cook to 375 degrees F.

In a large bowl, beat the egg, and then add the brown sugar, melted butter, and apple cider to the mix. Set that aside, and in another bowl, sift the flour, cinnamon, nutmeg, baking powder, baking soda, and salt together. Add the dry ingredients to the wet in thirds, mixing thoroughly along the way. Refrigerate the dough 30 minutes after it's all incorporated, then roll the dough out to 1/2 to 1/4 inch thick. Cut out your donuts and fry for 3 to 4 minutes, turning halfway through. Drain on paper towels, then add powdered sugar immediately, or wait until they're cool and add icing and sprinkles.

Makes 8–10 donuts and holes.

Donut Fluffs

We started calling these fluffs when our neighbor's child tried them at our annual Christmas party. The name stuck, and they've been fluffs ever since, but no matter what you call them, they are delicious!

Ingredients

- 2 eggs, beaten
- 1/2 cup granulated sugar
- 1/2 cup whole milk (2% or buttermilk may be substituted)
- 1 1/2 cups all-purpose flour
- 2 dashes salt
- 1 teaspoon nutmeg
- 1 heaping teaspoon baking powder
- 1½ to 2 quarts canola oil for frying (depending on the depth of your pot)

Directions

Heat the canola oil to 375 degrees F.

In a large bowl, beat the eggs first, and then add the sugar and whole milk. Set that mixture aside and sift together the flour, salt, nutmeg, and baking powder. Add the dry ingredients to the wet, stirring thoroughly as you go.

You can make small balls by using a pair of teaspoons, but we like to use a small cookie scoop to add the dough to the oil and cook for 2 to 3 minutes, turning the balls halfway through. Dust with powdered sugar or add icing after they are cool to the touch.

Makes about a dozen fluffs.

If you enjoy Jessica Beck Mysteries and you would like to be notified when the next book is being released, please send your email address to **newreleases@jessicabeckmysteries.net**. Your email address will not be shared, sold, bartered, traded, broadcast, or disclosed in any way. There will be no spam from us, just a friendly reminder when the latest book is being released.

Also, be sure to visit our website at jessicabeckmysteries.net for valuable information about Jessica's books.

OTHER BOOKS BY JESSICA BECK

The Donut Mysteries
Glazed Murder
Fatally Frosted
Sinister Sprinkles
Evil Éclairs
Tragic Toppings
Killer Crullers
Drop Dead Chocolate
Powdered Peril
Illegally Iced
Deadly Donuts
Assault and Batter
Sweet Suspects
Deep Fried Homicide
Custard Crime
Lemon Larceny
Bad Bites
Old Fashioned Crooks
Dangerous Dough
Troubled Treats
Sugar Coated Sins
Criminal Crumbs
Vanilla Vices
Raspberry Revenge
Fugitive Filling
Devil's Food Defense
Pumpkin Pleas
Floured Felonies

Short Stories in the Donut Mysteries
A Holiday Donut Steal

The Classic Diner Mysteries
A Chili Death
A Deadly Beef
A Killer Cake
A Baked Ham
A Bad Egg
A Real Pickle
A Burned Biscuit

The Ghost Cat Cozy Mysteries
Ghost Cat: Midnight Paws
Ghost Cat 2: Bid for Midnight

The Cast Iron Cooking Mysteries
Cast Iron Will
Cast Iron Conviction
Cast Iron Alibi
Cast Iron Motive
Cast Iron Suspicion

Made in the USA
Monee, IL
23 November 2020